A CHANCE FOR REVENGE

"Do I get to kill all of them?" Gates asked eagerly.

"All of them."

"Even the old marshal?"

"That's right," Carp said, "even the old marshal."

"What about Adams?" one of the other men asked.

"What about him?"

"He's got a reputation with a gun."

"So?" Carp asked. "There are enough of us to take care of him."

"I don't need any help," Gates said. "I can kill him by myself."

"Maybe you can," Carp said, "but we're gonna be there, so we might as well help."

"Okay," Gates said, "but I want the old marshal." Gates remembered how the marshal had made him back off the other day. "He ain't gonna have no gun under the desk this time."

*   *   *

This title includes a preview from *The Last Chance Kid* by Golden Spur Award–winning author Nelson Nye. *The Last Chance Kid* is on sale now from Jove Books.

THE GUNSMITH

122

THE STAGECOACH KILLERS

J. R. ROBERTS

JOVE BOOKS, NEW YORK

THE STAGECOACH KILLERS

A Jove Book / published by arrangement with
the author

PRINTING HISTORY
Jove edition / February 1992

ISBN: 0-515-10792-1

Jove Books are published by The Berkley Publishing Group,
200 Madison Avenue, New York, New York 10016.
The name "JOVE" and the "J" logo
are trademarks belonging to Jove Publications, Inc.

PRINTED IN THE UNITED STATES OF AMERICA

10 9 8 7 6 5 4 3 2 1

ONE

No matter how much trouble it got him into, Clint Adams had never ignored a call for help from a friend.

His friendship with John McIntyre went back many years, to when Clint Adams was a young deputy without a heavy reputation to tote around. In those days, the legend was just growing, but it didn't flower until the newspapers got ahold of it. As newspapers will, they exaggerated him into a full-fledged legend, and then the rumors started, and finally the dime novelists got ahold of him. He hadn't seen John McIntyre since he'd become the Gunsmith, but that didn't stop him from leaving his rig back in Labyrinth, Texas, saddling Duke, and heading for northern California—Sacramento, to be exact—the day after he received McIntyre's telegram.

He was going over some memories when he suddenly felt Duke take a bad step.

"Whoa, big fella, what's going on?" he asked, reining the big gelding in.

He dismounted and checked the bottom of each of Duke's hooves. On the front left hoof he found it, a blossoming bone bruise. He took a few steps back and found what he thought was the stone Duke had stepped on. It wasn't very big, but it had a point on it, and when Duke put his weight on it he bruised his hoof pretty bad.

"Hurts, doesn't it?" Clint asked Duke. He showed Duke the stone and then flung it as far as he could. "Well, big fella, I guess we walk from here on. Come on."

They started walking, and Duke was limping pretty good. There was no way Clint would ever do anything to hurt the big gelding, and he was ready to walk the last few miles to Sacramento, if he had to.

McIntyre was sitting at his desk when he saw, through the window, Dean Flood and two of his men walking toward his office. McIntyre frowned. He didn't remember ever disliking a man as much as he disliked Dean Flood.

He sat back in his chair and waited for Flood to enter the office.

Finally, the door opened. First one of his boys came in, then Flood, then the other bodyguard. Flood wore a gun in a shoulder rig, underneath whatever expensive suit he happened to be wearing that day, and rumor was he knew how to use that gun. Still, he never went anywhere without his bodyguards.

"Hello, John," Flood said.

"Flood."

At forty, Flood was eighteen years younger than McIntyre. McIntyre was the bigger man, though, standing six-four to Flood's six feet. Of the two, however, Flood was plainly in better shape. McIntyre had been toting around a burgeoning gut for the past ten years, while Flood was as trim and fit as a man could get. He took off the black, flat-brimmed hat he always wore and dropped it on McIntyre's desk. One of his men got a chair from the other side of the room and brought it over for Flood to sit in. He took a moment to light a slim cigar, and didn't even look at McIntyre again until he had it going to his satisfaction.

McIntyre was content to let Flood get to the point at his own pace, because he knew what his answer was going to be. It was the same answer he'd given the man the last dozen times he offered to buy him out.

The answer was no, and it would always be no.

"Heard you tried to buy a new axle yesterday," Flood said.

"So?"

"So, I heard you weren't allowed to buy it on credit. In fact, your credit's pretty bad in Sacramento, isn't it?"

"Ha!" McIntyre exploded. "If you know anything, you know my credit's pretty bad anywhere."

Flood smiled.

"Yeah, I do kinda know that, John."

"Maybe you even have somethin' to do with it, huh, Flood?"

"Me?" Flood said, innocently. He looked at his boys, who both smiled, and then back at McIntyre. "John, why would I want to damage your credit?"

"Come on, Flood," McIntyre said, becoming annoyed. "Let's not play cat and mouse. I hate playing cat and mouse, especially when some slick asshole thinks he's the cat and I'm the mouse."

The amiable look on Flood's face suddenly disappeared, and it was as if a dark cloud had settled over him. He narrowed his eyes and took the cigar out of his mouth.

"I've made my offer, old man," Flood said, "and it's a good one. I just came over to see if you were ready to accept it."

"Ain't ready now, and never will be," McIntyre said, "so take your hired muscle and get the hell out of my office."

"You gonna throw me out, old man?" Flood asked.

"You send your hired men outside and we'll see who throws who out, Flood. I may be old, but I can still handle the likes of you. Ain't never been the day I couldn't whip some tinhorn gambler."

"Now, John," Flood said, becoming amiable again, "you're getting all red in the face."

"Get out of my office, Flood."

Flood took his sweet time picking up his hat, cleaning it, and placing it on his head very carefully. He then put the cigar in his mouth and stood up.

"Think it over, John," Flood said. "This place is about to run itself into the ground. I can save it."

"Break it, you mean," McIntyre said.

One of the men took a step forward, eyeing McIntyre, and said, "Want me to teach him some manners, Mr. Flood?"

McIntyre cocked the .36 Navy Colt he'd been holding under the desk the whole time and said, "Try it, sonny, and I'll blow you a second belly button."

The man stopped short and frowned.

"Well, go ahead, Gates," Flood said in disgust, "teach the old man some manners."

Flood turned and headed for the door, followed by his first bodyguard. The second one, Gates, was still glaring at McIntyre.

"One day soon, old man, you won't have that gun."

"Get out of my office, punk," McIntyre said, "before I kill you just to keep my hand in."

Gates, not yet twenty-five, sneered at the old man, then turned and followed his boss.

McIntyre eased down the hammer on the Colt, laid it on the top of his desk, then took a bottle of whiskey from the bottom drawer. He uncapped the bottle, meaning to take one swallow. There was half a bottle left, and when he lowered the bottle it was empty.

Part of my damned problem, he thought, throwing the bottle across the room, where it struck the corner of the wall and shattered.

TWO

Outside, Gates caught up to Flood and the other man, whose name was Carp.

"He made a fool out of you, Gates," Flood said.

"If he didn't have that gun, Mr. Flood—"

"Never mind."

"What do we do now, boss?" Carp asked. Carp was in his thirties, sandy-haired, with a droopy mustache he thought covered a weak upper lip. It didn't.

"There's a stage due in in about three hours, isn't there?"

"That's what you said this morning, boss," Carp said. "You had the schedule."

"Yeah," Flood said, "There's a stage due in today—only I don't want it to get in, do I, boys?"

Gates and Carp exchanged a glance and then Carp said, "Hell, no, boss, you sure don't."

Flood rotated the cigar in his mouth for a moment, then took it out and said, "Deal with it."

"I'll be at the Lucky Deuce," Flood said, which was the

gambling hall and saloon that he owned. "Find me there and let me know how it went."

"Okay, boss."

"Carp," Flood said as the two men started off.

"Yeah, boss?"

He pointed at Carp with his cigar and said, "Don't mess up."

When Clint came to the road he thought that the chances of flagging down a coach might be pretty good. The road was obviously well traveled, and Sacramento was a pretty big town. Hell, it was a damned city, sort of a smaller version of San Francisco. He had ever heard that Sacramento had its own Chinatown.

He and Duke started walking the road, and a couple of hours later his optimism was rewarded. From behind him he heard the sound of an approaching stagecoach. He moved Duke off the road, then turned and started to wave, hoping the stage would stop.

It did.

"You lookin' to rob us, you're shit outta luck," the driver said. He was a grizzled old-timer who looked as if he'd been holding the reins of some team or other for about fifty years.

"Not looking to rob you," Clint said, "but I am looking for a ride."

"With a fine-looking animal like that under you?"

"Stepped on a stone a ways back," Clint said. "He's got a bruise and I don't want to push him."

"Don't blame you," the driver said. "Wouldn't want to do no damage to a good-lookin' animal like that. Well, you got yerself a ride, young feller, but you'll hafta ride up here with me. I'm full up."

"No problem," Clint said, "I'll just tie my horse to the

back of the coach." Duke could handle it okay.

Clint took care of that and then walked to the front of the coach to climb aboard. A brief look inside told him that the driver had been right. He was filled up, all right. There was a young boy looking out the window, and Clint tousled his hair as he went by. The woman next to him, in her late thirties and not especially pretty, must have been his mother.

Clint climbed aboard and said, "You riding without a shotgun?"

"Got nothin' of value," the old man said, whipping the team into action, "bu. I wouldn'ta had a shotgun, anyway. Company cain't afford one."

"Hard times?"

"The hardest," the man said. "We're down to one coach and team—this one—and one driver—me. Name's Purdy."

"Clint Adams," Clint said.

"Pleased ta meetcha," Purdy said, giving no indication that he might have recognized the name.

Clint sat back and watched the man work. Purdy might have been sixty—or seventy, or even eighty—but it didn't look as if his hands had lost any of their dexterity. He handled a team like nobody Clint had ever seen before, including himself.

"I admire the way you drive."

"You drive?" Purdy asked.

"I got a team and rig I usually travel with. Not this time, though."

"What kind of rig?"

"Peddler's rig I bought cheap years ago. Got myself a gunsmith shop in the back."

"That how you make yer money? Fixin' guns?"

"That's it."

"Got me a shotgun could use some work. Trade ya for the ride?"

"You got a deal, Purdy. We get into Sacramento I'll have a look at it for you."

Purdy laughed—actually, it was more of a high-pitched cackle than a laugh—and said, "Done deal."

Purdy went back to his driving, and Clint back to watching him. At the very least he could learn something about handling a team.

THREE

"Tarnation!"

Clint looked at Purdy and said, "What's the matter?"

"I don't think them fellers is lookin' for a ride," Purdy said, jerking his chin. "Do you?"

Clint looked to where the old man's chin had pointed and saw four men riding toward the coach from off the road.

"Robbers?" Clint asked.

"Looks like," Purdy said. "This ol' team ain't got much left, but I guess we're about to find out."

Purdy whipped the team into a gallop, and all six horses responded nicely. Clint could see what Purdy meant, though. Just by looking at the horses he could tell that they would tire soon.

"You wanna throw some shots their way?" Purdy asked. "Ya know, just to show them we ain't defenseless?"

It occurred to Clint that had he not gotten a ride, the coach *would* be defenseless. All he'd wanted was a ride to Sacramento, and now he was being drafted into duty as the shotgun guard.

As he drew his gun it also occurred to him that none of the four men had made any kind of a threatening gesture, other than simply riding toward the coach.

"You waitin' for them to shoot first?" Purdy shouted.

"As a matter of fact," Clint said, "yes."

At that point there was a shot, and a bullet struck the side of the coach near Clint.

"Glad I could arrange it for ya," Purdy called.

Clint fired back, and now all four men were firing at them with rifles.

They rode hard for a mile or so, and Clint started to notice something.

"They're not getting any closer," he said to Purdy.

"What?"

"The team is tiring, but those fellas are not getting any closer," Clint said again. "Also, they're using rifles, and staying out of range of my gun."

"I ain't got a rifle to give ya!"

That wasn't the point. The point was if these men were robbers, they weren't trying real hard to catch the coach.

"Goddamn!" Purdy shouted, and Clint turned his head to see what was happening. Before he could focus, however, he was thrown from the coach. Even as he was flying through the air, he wondered what the hell was going on.

He lost consciousness when he hit the ground.

Flood turned the redhead around so that her naked butt was staring him in the face. He got up on his knees, took hold of her hips, and drove himself into her. She gasped, and then began to moan as he pounded into her. He reached around to pinch her nipples, and his weight fell on her. She was a big girl, though, and able to handle it. He squeezed her big breasts, then took his weight on his knees again. Holding her by the hips, he pulled her to him as he drove into her, and she reached blindly for the bedpost and held on tightly.

"Yes, goddammit, yes," she shouted, "oh, Flood, you're so good . . ."

When he was done with her he turned her over and slapped her in the face.

"Jesus!" she said, putting her hand to her cheek. "What was that for?"

"The whore talk," he said, sitting on the bed and reaching for a cigar. "I told you before, don't use your whore talk on me."

"What whore talk?"

"All that 'you're the best' crap," he said, lighting the cigar. "Save that for your johns."

She rubbed her cheek, which had begun to redden, and said, "I don't take johns anymore."

"You will if I say so."

She dropped her hand from her cheek and put it on his shoulder.

"I'm sorry, Flood."

He turned his head and looked at her. She was twenty-eight—at least, that's what she admitted to. She had a mass of red hair that was naturally curly, a pale complexion dotted with freckles, and a fairly pretty face. Her body, however, was spectacular. She had large, firm breasts, big hips, and as fine a butt as he had ever seen on a woman—and Flood considered himself a fine judge of women. Her name was Judy Davis.

"Judy," he said, "go and get me a bottle of whiskey, will you?"

"Sure, Flood."

She stood up and pulled on a robe. He knew that if he told her to go downstairs to the saloon naked and get the bottle, she would do it.

When she returned with the bottle he uncapped it and took a healthy swig. As he lowered it he picked up his watch from the table near the bed and looked at it.

"Are you still after the stage line?" she asked.

He raised his eyebrows and said, "Why?"

"I just don't know why you want it," she said. "Sacramento's too big for you to waste your time on a stage line. God, we've got the railroad, and the docks, and Wells Fargo. Why do you bother yourself about a small, broken-down stage line?"

"You really don't know, do you?"

"No, I don't."

Flood picked a fleck of tobacco off his tongue, then took another drink. She stared at his body once again, admiring how there wasn't an ounce of fat on him. He wasn't a big man. In fact, she was almost taller than he was—she *was* taller than him when she was wearing her heels. She was used to being with bigger men, when she slept with men for her own enjoyment. She had never been with a man like Flood, though. He had confidence in himself that she had never found in anyone before.

"When I made my first offer, it was a lark," Flood said. "I own a saloon and gambling hall, I own several other businesses, and I thought it would be . . . interesting to own a stage line."

"So if it was a lark, why are you so obsessed with getting it now?" She took the whiskey bottle from him and took a drink.

"Because," he said, "that old man, McIntyre, said no to me."

"So?"

He took the bottle back.

"If you know anything about me by now, Judy," he said, "you know that I don't like to be told no."

She knew that for a fact—and she had seen what he did to people he didn't like.

"So just because he told you no—"

He turned to face her, his right hand coming up and cupping her face painfully.

"There's no such thing as *just* no, Judy," he said. "Nobody tells me no. It simply is not done. Do you understand?"

"Sure, Flood, sure," she said, "I understand."

She put her hand on his arm and ran it down to the hand that was holding her face. She tried to slide her hand into his, and he resisted for a moment, then relaxed his hand and released her face. She held the hand and brought it to her lips.

"I'd never say no to you, honey," she said, her lips against his hand.

He slid his hand from hers and ran it over her shoulder, down to her right breast. He hefted it lighty, then squeezed it.

"No," he said, putting aside the bottle, "I know you wouldn't. . . ."

FOUR

Clint came awake slowly. He was aware of some pain in his left shoulder, and a pounding headache. He reached behind him and found a small bump on the back of his head. When he touched it, the headache increased.

Slowly, he sat up and tried to collect his thoughts. He had been on a stagecoach . . .

Then he remembered.

He looked around quickly, then regretted it. Quick movements were not well received by his headache. This time, he looked around more slowly.

The coach was about fifty yards from him, lying on its side. All six of the team horses were gone. Carefully, he got to his feet and staggered over to it. The first thing he saw was a child's arm sticking out from beneath the wagon. He remembered the boy he had seen in the coach. He leaned over and took hold of the boy's wrist but could find no pulse.

"Damn . . ." he said.

He hated to do it, because it put more pressure on the boy's arm, but the lad was beyond feeling it. He climbed atop the coach to look inside. From what he could see, there were five people inside, and they were all dead.

He opened the coach door and lowered himself inside. Apparently the boy had been killed when the coach fell on him. That couldn't be said for everyone else in the coach, however.

The rest of the people, including the boy's mother, had been shot.

"Shit!" he said, beneath his breath.

He climbed out of the coach and began to look for Purdy. He found him about twenty yards away. He was lying on his side. As Clint started to lift him, the man's head flopped over on his broken neck.

"Aw, Purdy," Clint said. He'd know the man for only a matter of minutes, not even hours, and he had liked him.

"What the hell—" Clint said, standing up.

He walked back to the coach and climbed inside again. All of the passengers—four men, a woman, and a boy— still had their valuables, so the four men had not been robbers. They had been murderers, pure and simple.

And how had he escaped their killing spree? Possibly the fact that he had landed fifty yards from the coach, and they hadn't seen him.

Seven people dead, the coach damaged, and the team run off. Clint especially felt the deaths of Purdy and the boy, but he felt them all. From what he could see, their deaths were pointless.

Suddenly he thought of Duke. He looked around, wondering if the big gelding had been taken . . . or worse.

"Duke!" he shouted. "Hey, big fella?"

He started walking when suddenly he heard hoofbeats. He turned and saw Duke trotting up to him. There was a slight limp from the bone bruise.

"Hello, big boy," he said, patting the horse's neck affectionately. "It looks like you and I got pretty lucky, huh?"

He checked Duke out for injuries, but beyond the bone bruise he had none. He picked up the offending hoof and inspected it.

"Nope, can't ride you, not on that," Clint said, letting the hoof back to the ground.

Clint took a last look at the coach filled with dead people. There really wasn't any point in risking injury to Duke just to get to Sacramento faster. It didn't matter to the people in the coach or to Purdy. The four killers were long gone.

"Come on, big fella," Clint said, "we've got a little bit of a walk ahead of us."

Carp and Gates entered Flood's Lucky Deuce and looked around for him. They didn't spot him, so they walked to the bar.

"Two beers," Carp told the bartender, Jack Vance.

Vance brought the beers over and said, "You fellas been busy?" .

"Why do you ask?" Carp asked.

"You're both in a sweat," Vance said. "Hard riding?"

"Never mind," Carp said. "Where's Flood?"

"Where do you think?" Vance asked. "He's upstairs with Judy."

Carp looked at Gates, who smirked.

"That's where I'd like to be," Carp said.

"Haw," Gates said, "I have a woman like Judy every night."

"What?" Carp said.

"You heard me," Gates said. "I don't limit myself to one woman."

Now Carp exchanged a glance with Vance, who looked toward the ceiling.

"You expect us to believe that you have a different woman every night?" Carp asked.

"I got to," Gates said. "I got to have a woman every day."

Carp started to laugh.

"You don't believe me?"

"Of course I don't believe you," Carp said. "What would a woman like Judy see in you?"

"I give 'em what they want."

"Jesus, Gates," Carp said, shaking his head, "you're such a damned liar."

Gates was about to take offense when he Flood coming down the stairs.

"Hey, the boss is here," Gates said.

Carp turned and watched as Flood walked toward him. Flood was wearing a suit but no tie, and his white shirt was open at the collar.

"Beer, Vance," Flood said. He leaned his elbow on the bar, looked at his two men, and said, "Well?"

"We handled it," Carp said, "just like you wanted, boss. That stage won't be getting in on time."

"Good," Flood said, picking up his beer, "very good, Carp. All right, boys, have a good time now. Tell Eddie to give you fifty dollars each in chips . . . to gamble with, and good luck."

"Thanks, boss," Carp said.

Flood took his beer with him to his office.

"He's always givin' us money in chips," Gates said.

"He's not a fool," Carp said. "He knows he'll win it back that way."

"Not from me," Gates said. "I'm feelin' lucky tonight. I'm gonna break the bank."

"Yeah," Carp said as Gates headed for the faro table, "sure." He turned to Vance and said, "Fifty dollars in chips for twenty-five dollars in cash?"

Vance grinned, accepting the chips, and said, "As usual."

FIVE

I'm getting soft, Clint thought as he walked into Sacramento. There was a time a walk of a few miles wouldn't have started his feet hurting.

In his telegram McIntyre had instructed him to check into Sacramento Arms Hotel. Before doing that, though, he had to find a livery stable where Duke could get the proper treatment.

He stopped a man driving an impressive pair of horses, on the off chance that a man who drove horses like that would know how to take care of them. He asked for a livery stable he could trust, and was given directions. The man also told him that the stables were three blocks from the hotel.

Clint walked Duke to the livery and met the man in charge, Ray Lucas, who was very impressed with Duke.

"I ain't never had such an animal in my stable," Lucas said. "You can depend on me to take care of him."

"Are you sure you know how?"

Lucas was a bandy-legged man in his fifties with wispy gray hair and a lantern jaw.

"Hey, Mr. Adams," Lucas said, holding up his hands, "see those?"

He was showing Clint a missing finger on his right hand, and half of a missing finger on the left.

"Where do you think I lost those?"

In addition to the missing digit and a half, his hands were covered with the kind of scars that could only come from handling horses over the years. Horses were, at times, ornery animals, and it was not unusual for them to bite off a finger or two.

"Okay," Clint said, handing Duke over. "I'll be staying at the Sacramento Arms Hotel."

Lucas frowned and asked, "Why?"

"Why what?"

"Why are you staying there?"

"I'm supposed to meet a friend there."

"Who?"

"John McIntyre."

"I don't know him," Lucas said, "but there was a famous marshal by that name."

"It's the same man," Clint said. "He's retired, and I'm supposed to meet him there."

"Well, don't worry about this horse," Ray Lucas said, "I'll take care of him personally."

"I'll be back tomorrow, Ray."

"See ya then."

"Don't you want some money?"

"Ah, I'd work on a horse like this for nothin'," Lucas said, "but you can pay me after I'm finished."

"Deal," Clint said. "See you tomorrow."

Clint left the livery, carrying his gear, and walked to the

hotel. He signed the register and then ask the clerk if he knew a man named McIntyre.

"Sorry, sir, there's no one registered here by that name."

"No, I—never mind. Are there any messages for me?"

"I'll check." He looked in Clint's box and came out with a piece of paper.

"Thank you," Clint said. "Which way to the sheriff's office?"

"The police station is about five blocks away," the clerk said. "You go out the door, turn left, and keep walking."

"Thanks."

Clint went up to his room, wondering if he should find McIntyre first, or go and see the police. He opened the note, hoping that would make the decision for him.

"Come to the office of the Gold Stage Line," the note said. It was signed "John McIntyre."

Clint frowned. The stage he'd hitched a ride on had "Gold Line" written on the side of it—although the writing was somewhat faded.

Still, this helped him make up his mind. He refolded the note and left the hotel to find the Gold Stage Line, wondering what the hell John McIntyre had to do with it.

After asking several people, someone finally knew where the office of the Gold Stage Line was. When Clint got there, he could see why no one had known right away. To say that the place was run down was an understatement. Clint could believe what Purdy had said about the line only having one team, one coach, and one driver left—and now it didn't even have those.

He approached the door and knocked, then opened it. When he stepped inside, the place was empty. There was dust all over the place, except for the desk, which had been cleaned off. There was another door in the back wall, and Clint walked to it and shouted, "Hello! Anybody here?" When nobody answered he shouted, "John McIntyre!"

There was still no answer, so he turned and looked at the desk. To the left, against the wall, was a potbellied stove, with a coffeepot on top. Hanging from the stove by a chain was a tin coffeecup. That's when Clint knew that McIntyre was here. In all the sheriff's and marshal's offices that John McIntyre ever had, there was a tin cup hanging from a chain near the coffeepot. He always said it kept people from stealing the cup after they had a cup of coffee.

Clint walked to the pot and found that it was hot, so he poured himself a cup. As he was about to take his first sip a woman walked through the front door. She stopped short when she saw him.

"What are you doing here?" she asked.

"I'm having a cup of coffee," he answered. "What are you doing here?"

She gave him a hard stare, which was almost impossible given the kind of eyes she had. She was blond, with big brown eyes and a Cupid's bow mouth. Although she could have passed for twenty-nine, Clint guessed she was at least five or six years older than that. Still, she'd probably be able to pass for twenty-nine for another five years.

"I'm looking for John," she said.

"So am I."

"John Mills?" she asked.

He grinned and said, "No, miss, John McIntyre. Maybe you have the wrong office."

"I have the right office," she said. "Do you have business with Mr. McIntyre?"

"I do."

"Well then, would you tell him that Miranda was here?"

"Miranda who?"

"Miranda Ro—he'll know who. Just tell him Miranda, please."

Hew raised his coffeecup to her and said, "I'll tell him."

She stared at him for a moment, then turned and left. He sipped the coffee again, then put it down. It was so vile that he knew he had the right place. Nobody in the world made worse coffee than John McIntyre.

SIX

Clint was sitting at the desk when the door opened and John McIntyre walked in. Well, actually, he staggered to the door under the weight of a wagon wheel, leaned it against the outside wall, and then walked in.

"You still make the worse coffee I ever tasted," Clint said.

"Yeah," McIntyre said, "but at least you couldn't steal the cup."

McIntyre, a big bear of a man, strode to the desk as Clint held his hand out. Instead of taking the hand, McIntyre came around the desk and locked Clint into a bear hug, lifting him off his feet.

"Hey, you're going to break my ribs," Clint complained, but McIntyre ignored him and kept hugging him, then set him down and slapped him on the back.

"When did you get here?" McIntyre asked.

"A little while ago," Clint said. "I had to walk in because Duke picked up a stone bruise."

"Duke?"

Clint forgot that when he last saw McIntyre he hadn't yet partnered up with Duke.

"My horse."

"You named your horse?"

"So?"

"I just could never see naming something you might someday have to eat."

"Never mind," Clint said. "Uh, John, I have some bad news for you."

"Worse than this?" McIntyre said, waving his arms to indicate the office. "Bet you never expected to see me in my own business."

"How did you get into it, anyway?"

"Hell, I won it in a poker game," McIntyre said. "I returned a few years ago, and traveled around for a couple of years, but my butt ain't what it used to be. When I won this place I decided to come here and see what I won."

"And this is it?"

"This is it," McIntyre said, "but it ain't so bad. I've still got one coach, and one team, and one driver."

"That's what I wanted to talk to you about," Clint said.

"What?"

"Well, after Duke picked up the stone bruise I hitched a ride with a coach."

"My coach brought you in? Why didn't you say so? Where's Purdy?"

"John," Clint said, "Purdy's dead."

"Whataya mean, he's dead?"

"Purdy, and all the passengers," Clint said.

"What happened?"

"We were attacked by four men, and before I knew it I was flying through the air. When I came to, the coach was on its side, everyone was dead, and the team was gone."

"Robbers?"

"I'm afraid not," Clint said. "All the bodies still had their belongings on them. Also, there was a small boy on the coach."

"He dead, too?"

"They were all dead, John," Clint said. "The boy, his mother, and four male passengers."

"Sonofabitch!" McIntyre said. "Flood is crazy."

"Who's Flood?"

"He's the yahoo wants to buy this place from me," McIntyre said.

"Good," Clint said. "Sell it to him."

"I won't," McIntyre said. "I've turned him down a dozen times, and now he does this."

"Whoa, hold on, John," Clint said. "You were a lawman long enough to know you can't accuse somebody of murder without proof."

"Proof," John said, "Flood's way too smart to leave proof."

"Look," Clint said, "I have to go and talk to the police. Since the stage was yours, you'd better come with me."

"Damn right, I'll come with you," McIntyre said, "and then we'll go and see Flood."

They started for the door and then Clint said, "Oh, yeah, before I forget, there was a woman here looking for you."

"A woman. Who?"

"A very pretty brown-eyed blonde. She said her name was Miranda."

"Miranda Ross."

"A little romance blooming there, John?"

"Don't be an ass," McIntyre said. "She's my partner in this place."

"Partner?" Clint asked. "You have a partner in . . . this?"

"Sure," McIntyre said. "She owns forty-nine percent of the business."

"How did she get forty-nine percent?"

"The question is, how did I get fifty-one percent?" McIntyre said.

"You said you won it in a poker game."

"I did," McIntyre said, going out the door. "From her father."

SEVEN

On the way to the police station, McIntyre explained.

"Miranda used to help her father run the business, but all of a sudden the old man decided he wanted to travel, to see the country. She decided to try to keep the business going without him.

"His name was Charlie Ross, and I ran into him in Denver. We got into an all-night poker game, and by the time the sun came up ol' Charlie was tapped out, only he and I were in a hand that he didn't want to give up. He had no money, so he told me he'd put up his stage line business here in Sacramento. He wrote me a note saying that I was owed what he owned—if I won the hand, of course."

"And you did."

"He put an awful lot of faith in three kings. I had a straight. Anyway, when I got here I found out that Miranda owned forty-nine percent, and my piece of paper was worth fifty-one."

"How did Miranda feel about that?"

"We're still going 'round and 'round on that one," McIntyre said.

"Tell me about Flood."

"Well, he made an offer to Miranda to buy the place, and she said no. Once I arrived on the scene, as senior partner, he started making offers to me."

"And you started turning him down."

"And Flood don't take to being turned down."

"And you think he'd go this far, murder a stagecoach full of people, just to get your stage line?"

"People have killed for less," McIntyre said. "You've seen it, and I've seen it, too."

Clint had to admit, he'd seen people kill for a hell of a lot less.

When they reached the police station Clint said, "You know anyone in here?"

"I haven't had the pleasure."

They went inside and presented themselves at the front desk. Standing behind it was a uniformed policeman who asked if he could help them.

"My name is John McIntyre," McIntyre said, "I own the Gold Stage Line."

"Yes?"

"I want to talk to someone in authority."

"About what?"

"My coach was hit."

"Hit by what?" the young policeman asked.

"It was attacked."

"By who?"

"Son, if I knew that, I wouldn't be here," McIntyre said, becoming exasperated.

"Take it easy, John," Clint said. "Look, officer, the coach was attacked by four men, and everyone on it was killed. Could we talk to someone about that?"

"Why didn't you say that in the first place?" the policeman asked. "You want to talk to someone about a murder.
Have a seat and someone will be right with you."

There were some benches against the wall in front of the
desk, and Clint and McIntyre went and sat on one.

"Policemen," McIntyre said with disgust. "Give me a
sheriff or a deputy any day. Look at the idiots they're putting
uniforms on and calling policemen."

"We're not in the unsettled West now, John," Clint said.
"This is a city, and it has city law. It's almost like San
Francisco now, only smaller."

"Never been to San Francisco," McIntyre muttered, "and
don't ever want to go. Sacramento's a big enough city for
me."

They waited about ten minutes when a man came out
to talk to them. He was dressed in civilian clothes, a suit
with a vest, and a bowler hat. He took the hat off as he
approached them.

"You always wear a hat indoors?" McIntyre asked.

"John," Clint said.

The man, in his late thirties or so and sporting a big,
brush mustache, smiled and said, "I was just on my way
out, sir, when you came in. My name is Inspector Watson.
You said something about a murder?"

"My friend here can tell you more about it than I can,"
McIntyre said. "He was there."

Briefly, Clint told the inspector about hitching a ride
on the coach, and about the coach being attacked by four
men.

"You didn't actually see who shot them, though?" the
inspector said.

"No," Clint said, "but they're dead just the same."

"I'll have to take some men out to the scene to take a
look. We'll bring a wagon so we can bring the bodies back.

Mr. Adams, I'd like you to go with us so you can show us
where the location is."

"It's getting dark—"

"We'll be ready to leave in fifteen minutes. If it gets
too dark, we'll have lanterns along. I don't want to leave
those bodies out there overnight. There are two-legged and
four-legged jackals out there."

"I understand, sir," Clint said. "I'll be ready. I'll need to
get a horse. Mine came up lame."

"Yes, so you said," the inspector said. "We will supply
you with a horse. If you'll just wait here, please?"

"Sure."

As the inspector walked away, McIntyre said, "Did you
hear the way he said, 'so you said'?"

"So?"

"It sounded like he didn't believe you."

"He'll believe me when he sees the coach, John."

"I suppose so."

"And while I'm away, do me a favor," Clint said.

"What?"

"Stay away from Flood."

"I'm gonna talk to him—"

"Wait for me," Clint said. "I don't want you facing Flood
alone."

McIntyre grinned and said to Clint, "Just like old times,
eh, boy?"

"Yes, John," Clint said, "just like old times."

Miranda Ross didn't know what to think.

First this old, retired marshal shows up claiming to own
the Gold Stage Line, and then she finds out that he won
her father's share from him in a poker game. When he
presented her with the note, she had recognized her father's
handwriting immediately.

She had heard of Marshal John McIntyre, but she'd never expected to ever become partners with him. At first she was against it, but then she realized that McIntyre—although a little over the hill—might be just the man she needed to stand up to Flood and keep her business going.

What she hadn't expected, however, was for him to bring in any of his old cronies. She didn't know how to feel about that. She supposed she was going to have to wait and talk to McIntyre about the man she had seen drinking coffee in the office.

Not that he wasn't good-looking . . . in a rustic sort of way.

EIGHT

Clint and the inspector rode out on horseback, while two uniformed officers rode on a buckboard. It was twilight when they left, and Clint was able to find his way to the site of the massacre. It helped that all they had to do was follow the main road north out of Sacramento.

When they reached the site, the inspector had the two officers inspect it.

"It's just as he says, Inspector," one of the men reported. "Five dead in the coach, and the little boy."

"The driver's over there, sir," the other man reported. "His neck is broken."

"There are fresh bullet holes on the coach," the first man said.

"All right," Watson said. "Light the lamps and start moving the bodies onto the buckboard. I want them checked for valuables at the same time."

"Yes, sir."

"I can help—" Clint started.

"No, sir," Watson said, "I prefer that you stay here and talk with me."

"All right."

"Let's dismount."

They both stepped down from their horses and moved close to one of the lighted lamps. The inspector took out a slim cigar and offered Clint one. When Clint refused, the inspector lit his and didn't speak until he had it going to his satisfaction.

"Tell me again."

"Tell you what again?" Clint asked.

"All of it," Watson said, "slowly."

Clint studied Watson for a moment, and thought he detected suspicion on the man's gaze. He told the story again—slowly—from beginning to end, and Watson simply smoked his cigar and listened.

"Is that all of it?"

"Oh, yeah," Clint said. "Purdy said he had a shotgun he wanted me to fix."

"That's not relevant."

"Well," Clint said, "you said you wanted everything."

"You know what I find . . . remarkable?" Inspector Watson said.

"No," Clint said, "what do you find . . . remarkable, Inspector?"

"Well . . . now, don't get me wrong, I'm just talking but . . . I find it remarkable that everyone else was killed, and you weren't hurt at all."

"I wouldn't say I wasn't hurt," Clint said. "I still have a headache, and a stiff shoulder. In fact, I was going to see a doctor when we get back to town."

"Well, that's good," Watson said. "I'd be interested in what the doctor has to say."

"Uh-huh," Clint said as the first body was placed in the buckboard. It was one of the men from the stagecoach. "Why?"

"As I said," Watson said, "there are . . . certain aspects of this incident that I find fairly . . . remarkable."

"Look, Inspector," Clint said, "when I decided to report this to the police, I certainly didn't expect to become a suspect."

"Uh-huh," Watson said, "I'm sure you didn't."

A second body was placed in the buckboard, another of the men from the coach. Clint suddenly realized that he was waiting for them to bring out the body of the boy.

"I was just hitching a ride," Clint said. "What motive would I have for killing all those people?"

"I don't know that, Mr. Adams," Watson said. "It's my job to investigate this from every angle."

"And to suspect everyone?"

"I understand you used to be a lawman, Mr. Adams," Watson said.

Clint narrowed his eyes and asked, "How did you know that?"

"Oh, I recognized your name, and the name of Marshal John McIntyre. You're both pretty famous."

At that point three of the men and the woman had been placed in the buckboard.

"Uh, Inspector?" one of the men said.

"Yes?"

"We need some help, uh, getting the coach off the boy, sir?"

"I'll help," Clint said.

"We will both help," Watson said.

Clint and Watson helped one of the men lift the coach and hold it while the other man got the boy loose from inside. They dropped the coach and followed the man to the buckboard. He bumped the boy's arm as he was placing him on the buckboard next to his mother.

"Hey, easy!" Clint said.

"Sorry," the man said, sheepishly. He covered the bodies of the boy and his mother with a blanket and went to help the other man carry Purdy over. Clint moved to the buckboard and rearranged the blanket.

"You were never a detective, were you, Mr. Adams?" Watson asked.

"No, Inspector," Clint said, making sure the boy was completely covered, "I was never a detective."

"Well, if you were," Watson said, "you'd know that a detective's job is to suspect everyone."

"I thought a man was innocent until proven guilty," Clint said.

"By the courts, Mr. Adams," Watson said, "not by me."

Clint didn't speak with Watson the rest of the time out there. Once the bodies were loaded onto the buckboard and covered by blankets, Watson's men reported that all of the victims' valuables—wallets, jewelry, etc.—were present and accounted for.

"Well," Watson said, rubbing his jaw, "I guess that rules out robbery."

Good thinking, Clint thought. He wasn't sure if Watson was stupid—or just acted that way.

"Let's get these bodies to the undertaker's," Watson said. "Mr. Adams, I wonder if you'd come by the station in the morning so we can take a written report."

"Sure, Inspector," Clint said. "I'll be glad to help in any way."

"Thank you," Watson said. "Now, why don't we get back so that you can see a doctor."

• • •

When they returned to Sacramento, Clint went inside the police station with Inspector Watson.

"I want to thank you again for riding out there with us, Mr. Adams," Watson said.

"No trouble," Clint said.

"If you'd like me to recommend a doctor—"

"I'll just go and find my friend John McIntyre," Clint said. "I'm sure he'll have someone in mind."

"All right."

"I appreciate the offer, though."

"Certainly."

"Are you talking about the John McIntyre who owns the Gold Stage Line?" the policeman behind the desk asked. Clint noticed that it was not the same young man he and McIntyre had spoken to earlier. This one was older, more experienced, and a lot less stiff.

"That's right," Clint said.

"Would that be *Marshal* John McIntyre?"

"That's him."

The man looked impressed.

"I used to be a deputy when I was real young, and I always wanted to meet him. I'm sure sorry it had to be this way."

"What way?" Clint asked. "What are you talking about?"

"Yes, Officer," Inspector Watson said, "what are you talking about?"

"They brought Marshal McIntyre in here a couple of hours ago."

"For what?" Clint asked.

"He was arrested for murder," the policeman said. "Seems he killed a man named Flood."

NINE

"I told you not to go near him, John," Clint said. "Remember that?"

"I remember, I remember," McIntyre said, waving Clint away as if he were an annoyance. They were in McIntyre's cell, Inspector Watson having consented to let Clint talk to McIntyre while Watson looked into the case.

"All right," Clint said, "tell me what happened."

"There's nothin' to tell," McIntyre said. "I went to see him and he was dead."

"You took your gun with you, didn't you, John?"

"Sure I took my gun. I wasn't about to go into that saloon, filled with Flood's men, without a gun. I may have gotten old, but I ain't got stupid, yet."

"Well," Clint said, "not totally. The police say your gun was fired."

"Yeah, it was fired," McIntyre said. "Somebody shot at me, so I shot back."

"Who shot at you?"

"I don't know who shot at me."

Clint paused a moment to collect his thoughts, then went on.

"All right," Clint said, "tell me exactly what happened when you got to the saloon."

"I went in, I walked to the back where Flood's office was. I walked in without knocking. He was sitting at his desk. I started jawin' at him before I realized that he was dead."

"Dead how?"

"Whataya mean, dead how? He was dead. He'd been shot in the side of the head."

"You didn't see any blood?"

"The bullet went in, and it didn't come out," McIntyre said. "There wasn't much blood. I just noticed that he looked funny. He was sittin' up straight and his eyes were vacant."

"What happened then?"

"Well, I was gonna go and look at him, but then someone took a shot at me from the window."

"What window?"

"There's only one in the room," McIntyre said. "It's right behind his desk."

"Wasn't he in the way of anyone wanting to take a shot at you?"

"It ain't right behind his desk, it was a little to his left."

"How many shots were fired at you?"

"One."

"How many'd you fire back?"

"Two," McIntyre said. "Snapped 'em off real quick."

"Hit anything?"

"I don't know," McIntyre said. "Ask the police. They're the ones checked the alley."

"And that's all of it?"

"That's it."

"Did the customers hear the shooting?"

"They must've, because the door got flung open and there was the bartender, holding a shotgun on me. There was a bunch of people behind him, tryin' to see in."

"And then they called the police?"

McIntyre nodded and said, "Held me there at gunpoint until the police came. Listen, are you gonna get me out of here?"

"Not tonight," Clint said, "but I'll find a lawyer early in the morning."

"Don't get me just any lawyer," McIntyre said. "Get me a good one."

"I will."

"How? You don't know anybody in town."

"I know one person, other than you."

"Whozat?"

"I know Miranda Ross."

Clint met with Inspector Watson in his office.

"You've been in town one day, Mr. Adams, and already you're involved with two incidents of murder."

"Are you going to suspect me of this one, too?" Clint asked.

"Of course not," Watson said. "You were with me when it happened."

"How's the case against McIntyre look?"

"Airtight. He entered the saloon demanding to see Flood, making no secret of his anger. He entered the office without knocking, and then everyone heard a shot and rushed in."

"One shot."

"I don't have a written report on the incident yet, so I can't answer that."

"When will you take him before a judge?"

"We'll try and arrange it for tomorrow. You had better get your friend and a good lawyer."

"Are there any in town?"

"A few. Under the circumstances, I can't recommend one."

"I understand," Clint said. "I'll have to go elsewhere for that."

"About the other, uh, incident, you will come back in the morning to make a written statement?"

"I'll be here," Clint said, "to make a statement, and to get my friend out of jail."

Watson nodded, and Clint got up and left. As he was leaving, the officer behind the desk called him over.

"Are you, uh, the Clint Adams?"

"I'm Clint Adams."

"Geez," the man said, "two famous men in the station in one day. You worked with Marshal McIntyre years ago, didn't you?"

"That's right."

"Boy, what I would give to have worked with him."

"What's your name?"

"Evans, Joe Evans."

"How did you get this job?"

"I did some deputy work in Wyoming and Arizona. When I decided to come here, I applied for a job with the police department. These departments are gonna be all over the country one day, you know. Won't be no more sheriffs and deputies and such."

"Maybe not," Clint said. "Officer Evans, can you direct me to Hanover Street?"

"Sure thing. You can walk it if you like, but you should probably take a cab this time of night. Go out the front door and make a right. If you walk five blocks to Fourth Street . . ."

Clint noted the man's directions, then thanked him and left the station. He stepped into the street, hailed a horse-drawn cab, and told the driver to take him to Hanover Street.

"Smart man," the driver said, "Shouldn't walk it this time of night. . . ."

TEN

When Clint reached the house on Hanover Street where Miranda Ross lived, he walked to the door and rang the bell. McIntyre said that Miranda used to live here with her father, and that she despaired of not being able to continue the payments to the bank if the stage line failed.

When the door opened, Miranda Ross was standing there, holding a robe together with her right hand. Her tousled hair told him that he had gotten her out of bed. She looked so lovely that he couldn't help wondering if she had been in bed alone.

"What . . ." she said, rubbing her eyes with her left hand and then looking at him again. "Who are you?"

"We met earlier today, remember?" Clint said. "At the stage line offices?"

"Oh, yes," Miranda said, "but what are you doing here? How did you know where I live?"

"McIntyre told me."

"Well, what do you want so late?"

"I hope I didn't interrupt anything."

"Of course not," she said, lifting her chin. "I was asleep."

"Well, some things have happened that you should be aware of," he said. "Plus, I need your help."

"For what?"

"If you'll let me in," he said, "I'll tell you all about it."

She hesitated, holding her robe even more tightly, and then said, "Well, all right."

She allowed him to enter and closed the door behind them.

"Come this way."

She led him to the living room, which was tastefully furnished in subdued colors.

"Will we need coffee?" she asked.

"I think we will, yes," Clint said. He sat down and rubbed his own eyes.

"You look tired."

"I am."

"Before I go off and make coffee," she said, "don't you think I should know your name?"

"Didn't I tell you this afternoon?"

"If you did, I don't remember."

Neither did he.

"My name is Clint Adams."

"Miranda Ross."

"I know," he said, "John told me."

"John? Oh, Mr. McIntyre."

"Is that what you call him? He's your partner."

"I've only known him a short time," she said. "I'll get the coffee."

She left to go to the kitchen, and Clint put his head back for a minute.

●　●　●

She shook him awake later and said, "Here's your coffee."

"Jesus," he said, rubbing his eyes with the heels of his palms this time, "did I fall asleep?"

"You did," she said, sitting on a smaller chair across from him. There were two cups of coffee and a coffeepot on the table between them. "Why don't you tell me what's going on, so you can go to your hotel and get some sleep?"

He sipped the coffee, then told her everything, from the moment he hitched a ride with the coach up until his conversation with McIntyre in his cell.

"I can't believe all of this," she said, after having listened in silence. "Do you really think that Mr. Flood had those people killed?"

"I don't know," Clint said. "Right now my biggest concern is McIntyre."

"Did he kill Flood?"

"He says he didn't, and I believe him. What I need from you is the name of a lawyer."

A light seemed to go on in her eyes.

"I know a lawyer."

"Is he good?"

"He's very good."

"Can you get to him early in the morning?"

"Yes, I think so."

"Good," Clint said. "Have him meet me at the police station at nine o'clock."

"Nine?" she said. "If you're going to be up by then, you'd better get to your hotel and get to bed."

"Yes," he said, "you're right. Thanks for the coffee, and the nap on the sofa."

"I'll walk you to the door."

At the door she turned and said to him, "Will you be able to meet me at the stage office after the police station?"

"Sure. Why?"

"I think tomorrow I'll need your help," she said. "I'll have to hire someone to go out and get that coach, and to find our horses. That was the last team we had."

"There should be some extra teams at some of your stops."

"We're down to only one stop," she said, "but we can talk about that tomorrow. Can you meet me at eleven, Mr. Adams?"

"I don't see why not," he said, "but you'll have to call me Clint."

"All right," she said. "Are you, uh, a good friend of Mr. McIntyre's?"

"John and I go way back," he said. "Don't worry, I'll be around to help you both."

"Thank you," she said, smiling. "That makes me feel better."

"Good night, Miranda."

"Good night, Mr.—I mean, Clint."

He left her house and went in search of a cab to take to his hotel.

When he got back to his hotel he checked the desk for messages.

"None, sir," the clerk said. It was a different clerk from last time.

He was about to go upstairs when he stopped and asked the clerk, "How far away is the Lucky Deuce Saloon?"

"That's in the Square, sir."

"The Square?"

"Down near Center Street," the clerk said. "I can have a cab take you there, if you've a mind to gamble tonight. There are quite a few places in the Square."

"All right," Clint said, "I'll take you up on that. Get me a cab to the Square."

ELEVEN

The Square turned out to be a smaller version of San Francisco's famous Portsmouth Square. In San Francisco, all of the higher-class hotels and gambling casinos were in Portsmouth Square. Here in Sacramento it seemed they were trying for the same effect. As the cab drove him through the Square, Clint saw the Lucky Deuce, the High Spade, the Little Alhambra, the Faro House and several others. He had the cab drop him right in front of the Lucky Deuce.

When he entered, he found the place in full swing. The murder of the boss hadn't seemed to hurt business any. The bar ran the entire length of the left wall. Against the right wall were several faro and roulette tables. Strategically placed were poker and blackjack tables. The floor was being worked by about half a dozen girls. If this place were in Portsmouth Square, the other halls would probably try to close it down. This was simply a larger version of a Dodge City or Deadwood saloon.

Clint walked to the bar and ordered a beer.

When the bartender brought it he paid for it and said, "Too bad about your boss."

"That goin' around already?" the bartender asked.

"I've only been here a day and I heard about it," Clint said. "Looks like it hasn't hurt business any, though."

"Shit, no," the bartender said, "they're comin' out of the woodwork. They even want to see where it happened."

"I wouldn't think a killing would attract so much attention."

"Ain't so much the killing as who done the killing."

"Who was that?"

"A famous man," the bartender said. "Ever hear of Marshal John McIntyre?"

"Sure," Clint said. "He's the one who did it?"

"The very one."

"Well," Clint said, "that would attract attention. How many people saw him do it?"

"Huh?"

"I assumed that there were witnesses."

"Uh, no, no witnesses," the bartender said.

"Then how do you know he did it?"

"Well, we heard the shot and I grabbed my shotgun and ran into the office, right back there."

"That door there?"

"Yep. McIntyre was standing there with his gun smoking, and the boss—that's Mr. Flood—he was sittin' behind his desk, shot through the side of the head."

"The side of the head?"

"That's right."

"And McIntyre was standing in front of him?"

"That's right."

"Sounds like some pretty fancy shooting, to me."

"How do you mean?"

"Well," Clint said, using his thumb and forefinger as a

gun, "if McIntyre was standing in front of Flood, how did he manage to shoot him in the side of the head?"

The bartender frowned and said, "I don't know nothin' about that. All I know is that the police took him away and charged him with murder."

"I see."

"You want to see the office?"

"Sure," Clint said. Then he added, "How much?"

"A dollar."

"It's worth it," Clint said.

He gave the bartender the dollar, and the man walked him to the back and let him into the office. Another man tried to peek inside, but the bartender pushed him away and said, "Pay your dollar like everyone else, Harry."

Inside, Clint took a quick look at the layout. It was just as he had pictured from McIntyre's story. With Flood seated at the desk, the window would have been to his left. At the moment, the window was closed.

"Is that window always closed?"

"I don't know," the man said. "Tell you the truth, I was hardly ever in here."

"Just Flood?"

"And Judy."

"Judy?"

"She was his woman. Judy Davis. Used to work the floor, but when Flood took over he took her off the floor and put her upstairs in his room. I don't know what's gonna happen to her now. Guess that's up to Mr. Martin."

"Martin?"

"James Martin," the bartender said. "He was Flood's partner in this place—and a lot of others."

This was the first Clint had ever heard of a James Martin.

"Martin ever come in here?"

"You kidding?" the bartender asked. "That would be slumming. He stays where the big money is. He lives high, Martin does."

"Why would he want a piece of this place, then?"

"I don't know," the bartender said. "You finished? I gotta get back to work."

"Sure," Clint said. "Thanks for giving me a look."

"Hey," the bartender said with a shrug, "you paid for it."

Clint followed the bartender out of the office and back to the bar. He wondered how he might get to talk to Judy.

"You supposed this Judy would be taking any customers?" he asked.

"I doubt it," the man said. "She's sort of in mourning, ya know? Hey, maybe tomorrow."

"Yeah," Clint said, "maybe tomorrow. Thanks again for the look around."

Clint went outside, got himself a cab, and went back to his hotel. He had to get some sleep if he was going to get up early in the morning.

After Clint left, Carp came over to Vance, the bartender.

"Who was that?"

"I don't know," Vance said. "Just a guy who wanted to see the office where Flood was killed."

"He looked like he had a lot of questions."

"Now that you mention it, he sure did," Vance said. "You know what else he wanted?"

"What?"

"He wanted to screw a dead man's woman."

"Judy?"

"Yeah."

Carp frowned.

"Maybe Mr. Martin would want to know about this."

"You got Martin's ear?" Vance asked in surprise.

"No," Carp said, putting his beer glass down, "but this could get it for me."

TWELVE

Clint showed up at the police station at five minutes to nine, hoping that Miranda would be able to reach her lawyer friend early enough. As he entered, there was a tall, well-manicured young man seated on one of the benches. He appeared to be about thirty years old. He stood up as Clint approached.

"Mr. Adams?"

"That's right."

The man stuck out his hand.

"My name is Jeffery Wolfe. Miranda Ross told me you needed a lawyer rather badly."

"Very badly," Clint said, sizing the man up. He was a little younger than Clint would have liked, but beggars couldn't be choosers. "Did she tell you what the problem was?"

"Murder," Wolfe said. "That's quite a big problem."

"Come on," Clint said, "let's see if we can get you to work on it."

They approached the desk and asked for Inspector Watson. When the inspector appeared, he surprised Clint by smiling and extending his hand. It took only a second for Clint to figure out that he wasn't the recipient of the smile, or the hand.

"Hello, Jeffery."

"Inspector Watson," Wolfe said, shaking the inspector's hand. "Good to see you."

"Always good to see you, my boy," Watson said. He looked at Clint and said, "I take it you've retained Mr. Wolfe as Marshal McIntyre's attorney?"

"Not yet," Clint said. "He's going to have to talk to the marshal first. McIntyre will decide if he wants him as a lawyer, and I guess Mr. Wolfe will decide if he wants the marshal as a client."

"Well, let's get them together and see what happens, hmm? Are you ready to give your written statement?"

"I'm ready, but I'd like to go with Mr. Wolfe—"

"If you don't mind," Wolfe said to both Clint and Watson, "I'd like to interview the marshal alone."

"No problem," Watson said.

"Well," Clint said, "I guess—"

"You can make your statement while Jeffery talks with the marshal."

"Fine," Clint said, dubiously.

Watson had an officer take Wolfe to see McIntyre, and took Clint into his office to make the statement.

When Clint was finished with his statement, Wolfe was nowhere to be found. Watson told him that the lawyer was still with "his client." Clint decided to leave the two of them be. He had promised to meet Miranda Ross at the stage line office.

•   •   •

When he reached the office, Miranda was already there. She was in the process of cleaning, broom in hand, sweeping the floor.

"Believe it or not," she said, "the place didn't always look like this. We had a break-in last week, and whoever it was really made a mess."

"McIntyre didn't tell me that."

"Well, it must have been Flood's men, because it was just after we turned down an offer." She stopped sweeping, leaned on the broom, and looked at him. "Did you meet Jeffery?"

"I did," Clint said.

"What did you think?"

"I'll reserve judgment," Clint said. "He was very well acquainted with Inspector Watson."

"Is that in his favor?"

"I'll reserve judgment on that," Clint said. "Have you ever heard off of a man named James Martin?"

"Of course," she said. "He's a very wealthy man."

"He was also partners with Flood."

She was about to resume sweeping and stopped to stare at him.

"What?"

"The way I figure it," Clint said, "Martin has certain business interests that he doesn't want anyone to know about. So he used Flood to buy them and manage them."

"So Flood wasn't the boss?"

"He was to everyone," Clint said, "but Martin."

"So what does that mean?" she asked. "Flood didn't have those people killed, Martin did? Flood doesn't want to buy us out, Martin does?"

"Could be."

She dropped the broom and said, "So our problems with

Flood aren't solved? We'll just have to deal with Martin now?"

"Or his new representative."

"And who is that going to be?"

"I don't know," Clint said, "but maybe I should go and ask him."

THIRTEEN

They left the office, and Miranda took Clint to a small restaurant, where they had coffee. On her recommendation he also had a piece of peach pie, which was excellent.

"Clint, this is a whole different matter now," she said when they were seated at a table.

"Why?"

"Why? Because it involved James Martin, that's why. We're talking about one of the most powerful men in Sacramento."

"Why is he so powerful?"

"Because he is," she said. "He's rich, he has ties to banks, railroads, politicians, you name it."

"Then why would he want a small stage line?"

"Because," Miranda said, "he always gets what he wants. Rich men are like that. They see something that someone else has, so they offer to buy it."

"And when they can't," Clint said, "they try to take it. I've run into men like that before."

"But never one like James Martin."

"Miranda," Clint said, frowning, "do you know James Martin personally?"

She looked away for a moment, then said, "Yes, Clint, I do."

"Well then," Clint said, "maybe we know why he wants it."

She didn't answer.

"Tell me where he lives," Clint said, "or where I can get in touch with him."

"Your best bet would probably be his offices," she said. "They're on Dumont Street. Martin Industries."

"Martin Industries," Clint repeated. "Shall I give him your regards?"

"Please," she said, "there's nothing I want to give him, not even that."

"I'm not going to pry," Clint said. "If and when you want to talk about it, I'll listen."

"Jeffrey will be coming by my house later today," she said. "You'd better be there, to talk about Mr. McIntyre."

"I'll be there," Clint said. "Is five all right?"

"I'll make dinner."

"I'd appreciate that," Clint said. "It's been a long time since I had a home-cooked meal."

"Don't thank me until you taste my cooking," she warned.

FOURTEEN

Clint had a cab take him to Dumont Street. He simply had it drop him on a corner, and then walked, looking for Martin Industries. He wanted to get a feel for the area, and the feel he got reeked of money. There were banks, savings and loans, investment houses, and windows that simply said "Somebody, Inc." or "Anybody Ltd.," and finally "Martin Industries."

The building was constructed of brick, and a large plate-glass window on the second floor bore the legend. He entered and ascended the stairs to the second floor. As he expected, he was confronted by a secretary, and a pretty one at that.

"Can I help you?"

She was young, in her early twenties, but had the disposition of a woman much older, much more mature. She had dark hair piled high upon her head, and her face was expertly made up. She was very lovely, full-figured, almost plump.

"My name is Clint Adams," he said. "I would like to see James Martin."

She folded her hands on the desktop, tilted her head to the left, and asked, "Junior or Senior?"

He took a moment to decide, and then said, "Junior." He figured if Miranda had had some kind of a relationship with one of them, it would have had to have been Junior.

"Is he expecting you?"

"No."

"What is your business, then?"

"Tell him it has to do with the death of a man named Flood."

"Oh," she said, and her face became totally unreadable. Up until that point there was a pleasant expression on her face, as she studied him with some interest. Suddenly her face was like stone, betraying nothing of what she was thinking. Clint guessed that she was a very good secretary.

"Please wait here," she said, standing up. He could see now how full-bodied she really was, with full, rounded breasts and hips. She could have been as much as fifteen pounds overweight, but on her it looked lovely.

He watched as she walked to a door, knocked, and entered. After a moment she came out and held the door open for him.

"This way, please."

He obeyed and walked past her, inhaling the scent of her perfume as he did. She smiled as he passed her, a smile full of invitation.

"Mr. Martin," she said, "this is Mr. Clint Adams."

The man in the office was standing behind his desk. His back was to the window, which overlooked the street. He was tall, in his thirties, with hair and beard a rust color. His eyes were green. He was wearing a banker's three-piece suit, and it fit him very well. Obviously, the man had his own tailor.

"Mr. Adams," he said, "I understand this is about the death of Mr. Flood?"

Clint heard the door close behind him, and walked toward the desk.

"Murder, Mr. Martin," Clint said. "Flood was murdered."

"Yes, that's what I understand," Martin said, "by an old marshal, I heard. Please, sit down."

Clint sat, and Martin lowered himself into his leather chair.

"Something of a legend in the Old West, isn't he?" Martin asked.

"Something like that," Clint said, "but I don't think he did it."

"Oh? Why not?"

"Because he says he didn't."

"Excuse me, Mr. Adams," Martin said, "but what murderer ever admits his guilt?"

"Mr. Martin," Clint said, "Flood was making an offer to Mr. McIntyre for the Gold Stage Line."

Recognition lit Martin's eyes.

"Ah, now I understand," he said. "McIntyre owns the other fifty-one percent of the stage line. He got it from Miranda's father, I understand."

"Yes."

"Would you mind if I asked how he got it?"

"He won it in a poker game."

Martin laughed and said, "I find that very funny."

"Here's something you won't find funny," Clint said. "I believe that Flood had four men ambush the stage and kill everyone on it."

"How do you know that?"

"I was on the stage at the time," Clint said. "I was thrown clear and knocked out. When I came to, I found everyone dead."

"You believe Flood is guilty of that. You don't know for a fact."

Clint hesitated a moment, then said, "Would a man admit to such a thing, Mr. Martin?"

"Certainly not," Martin said, "but neither would I put the blame on a man unless I had proof."

"Flood wanted to buy the line," Clint said. "Was he acting on your behalf?"

Martin did not seem inclined to answer that question.

"Let me ask you a question, Mr. Adams," he said. "What's your place in all of this?"

"McIntyre is my friend," Clint said. "I came here to help him."

"By the same token, does Miranda merit this help of yours?"

"She does."

"She's a lovely woman, isn't she?"

"Very."

"Did she say anything about her and . . . me?"

"She didn't."

"I see."

"I don't."

Martin laughed again.

"We grew up together," Martin said. "Her father and my father were friends at one time. A lot of people thought we'd get married when we grew up. Unfortunately, our families grew apart."

"Was the wedge that pushed them apart money?"

"You're an astute man," Martin said. "Yes. My father grew wealthy while Miranda's father grew . . . well, maybe he didn't."

"I see."

"I thought you might," Martin said. "You should also know that I still intend to marry Miranda."

"Miranda might have other ideas."

"Then she did say something," Martin said. His tone was accusatory.

"No," Clint said, "it was not so much what she said as what she didn't say."

Martin sat back and stroked his beard.

"I asked a question earlier," Clint said. "Was Flood representing you with his offer for the stage line?"

"Flood represented me with some of my holdings," Martin said. "The Lucky Deuce was one."

"Are you saying yes, or no?"

"I'm saying," Martin said, slowly, "that I'm not really inclined to discuss my business with you. In fact, I don't think we have anything more to discuss."

Clint stood up and said, "I intend to prove that Marshal McIntyre didn't kill Flood, Mr. Martin. That means I will have to find out who did."

"You're not a policeman," Martin said. "I don't believe I have to talk to you."

"No, you don't," Clint said, "but maybe I'll come back with a policeman."

Martin smiled condescendingly and said, "I think you'll find that won't do you any good, but you're welcome to try it."

The implication was that Martin—or Martin money, probably Martin, *Senior* money—owned the police.

"We'll see," was all Clint could muster at the moment.

Martin pressed a button on his desk, and Clint heard a faint buzzer. The secretary apparently heard it, too, for she opened the door. Handy item. Electricity was useful for a lot more than just creating light.

"Good day, Mr. Adams."

Clint turned and walked out into the outer office. The secretary closed the office door and said, "I'll see you to the door."

She walked with him to the door and opened it for him. As he started through it she put one hand on his chest and held a piece of paper out to him with the other.

"My address," she said. "You're a stranger in Sacramento. You might want someone to . . . talk to."

He took the paper and said, "Thanks."

She smiled, and closed the door behind her. He unfolded the paper. It had "Brenda Loring" written on it, and her address. He put it in his pocket and went down the stairs.

After Clint Adams left, James Martin, Junior sat behind his desk and pondered the situation. His ultimate goal in all of this was Miranda. If Clint Adams threatened to get in the way of that, he'd have to be eliminated.

Martin stood up and walked to a connecting door in the wall to his right. He knocked and then opened the door.

"Father," he said, "we have to talk. . . ."

FIFTEEN

Clint reached Miranda's house promptly at five. When he knocked he was surprised when the door was opened by Jeffery Wolfe.

"Come on in, old man," Wolfe said.

Old man?

"Where's Miranda?"

"She's preparing dinner," Wolfe said, leading Clint to the parlor. "I'm supposed to play the good host. Can I get you a drink?"

"Yes, thanks."

"Brandy?"

"Fine."

Wolfe moved about the room with familiar ease that for some reason set Clint's teeth on edge. He watched as the man poured a brandy and then brought it to him.

"Thanks," Clint said. "What happened with McIntyre?"

"The marshal is now my client," Wolfe said.

"Did you get him out?"

"It's not that easy," Wolfe said. "The judge set a very high bail."

"How high?"

"One hundred thousand."

"Jesus," Clint said, "that high."

"We can get him out by putting up a portion of it in good faith."

"How much of a portion?"

"Ten percent."

Clint pursed his lips and then said, "That's still ten thousand dollars."

"Have you got that much?"

"I can probably get it."

"Hear me out first," Wolfe said. He sat in the same chair Miranda had used the night before.

"About what?"

Wolfe crossed his right leg over his left knee and held his brandy snifter easily in his right hand. The man's face was clean of lines, and his hair was impeccably in place. In a few years he'd probably look the same way. When he was forty he'd probably still look thirty. Clint had to admit that he and Miranda made a good couple, even though he was younger than she was. They certainly made a better couple in his mind than she and Martin would.

"I think we should leave him in jail," Wolfe said.

"What?"

"I listened to his story very carefully," Wolfe said. "I think he's telling the truth."

"So why leave him in jail?"

"If he's telling the truth," Wolfe said, "then he's being framed."

"Right."

"If we get him out," the lawyer went on, "whoever framed him might try to kill him."

"I can protect him."

"Sacramento isn't your bailiwick, old boy," Wolfe said. "I submit that he'll be much safer in prison. If he's out, you won't be able to find out who really did it. You'll be too busy protecting him."

Clint frowned. He didn't like the way it sounded, leaving McIntyre in jail, and the old marshal would like it even less, but goddammit, it made sense.

"I'll talk to McIntyre."

"Oh, he won't like it," Wolfe said, "but make him see that it's the right thing to do. I'm sure you can do it. He thinks quite a bit of you."

At that moment Miranda came into the room.

"Clint, hi," she said.

"Hello, Miranda."

Wolfe sprang from his seat and poured her a brandy.

"Here you are, dear," he said.

Clint winced at the word "dear." Wolfe might be a good lawyer—and that still remained to be seen—but he wasn't quite Clint's kind of man.

"Are you ready for dinner?" Miranda asked Clint.

"I'm starved."

"Good," she said. "We'll eat, and then you can tell us how it went with Mr. Martin."

"Yes," Wolfe said, putting a possessive arm around Miranda's shoulder, "we're very interested in that."

Clint thought that she looked a bit uncomfortable with Wolfe's arm around her, but it may have been something he wanted to see.

"This way to the dining room," she said, and broke away from Wolfe's arm to lead them there.

• • •

Miranda was unfortunately right about her cooking, but at least it was hot and, while it was not wonderful, it was still edible.

"How was it?" she asked him.

Before Clint could speak, Wolfe said, "You can tell her the truth. I've already told her many times what a bad cook she is."

Wolfe's subtle way of telling Clint that he had been here for dinner many times before.

"It was fine, Miranda," Clint lied, "just fine."

"His taste buds must be dead," Wolfe said.

"Never mind," Miranda said. "If he says he liked it, he liked it."

She got up and started clearing the plates.

"Let me help," Clint said.

"Oh, no," she said, "I'll take care of it. You and Jeffery go back into the parlor and have another brandy. I'll bring coffee out."

"Come on, Clint," Jeffery Wolfe said, clapping him on the shoulder is a grand gesture of comradeship, "there's no point in arguing with her. I've tried many times."

Wolfe led the way out of the dining room, and as Clint followed him he thought, no, sir, Jeffery, there is just no way you and I are ever going to be friends.

SIXTEEN

In the parlor Wolfe offered Clint another glass of brandy.

"I'll wait for the coffee, if it's all the same to you," Clint said.

"Have it your way, old man."

"Uh, look, Jeffery, I'd really rather you didn't call me that."

"Call you what?" The look on Wolfe's face was one of total innocence.

"Old man," Clint said. "I really don't like it. It's sets my teeth on edge. In fact, Jeff, you sort of set my teeth on edge."

Wolfe turned, and holding a brandy snifter in his hand, looked at Clint.

"Really?" He seemed puzzled. "Why?"

"You have an attitude," Clint said. "Haven't you ever noticed?"

"What kind of attitude?" Wolfe asked. "Hey, this is interesting, you know? No one's ever spoken to me like that before."

"Yeah, well," Clint said, "maybe somebody should have—maybe when you were growing up."

"You mean, like my parents?"

"Yeah, for a start."

"Well, my parents hardly ever spoke to each other, let alone to me," Wolfe said. "I always had to fend for myself, you know? Sort of raised myself."

"Yeah, well," Clint said, grudgingly, "I suppose that's to be admired."

"Really?" Wolfe asked, that innocent look creeping onto his face again. "I hadn't really thought about it that way."

"Jeff—"

"Oh, Clint," Wolfe said, "I'd really rather you didn't call me Jeff. My name is Jeffery."

"Really?" Clint said. "How about that . . . Jeff?"

Wolfe eyed Clint for a few moments and then said, "You know, I think I understand what you mean."

"About what?"

"About me setting your teeth on edge."

They were staring at each other when Miranda entered the room with a tray of coffee.

"What's going on?" she asked.

They both looked at her and Clint said, "We're just establishing some ground rules . . . right, Jeffery?"

"That's right . . . Clint."

"Well," Miranda said, "thank God for that. Let's have some coffee."

Over coffee Clint told them how his meeting with Martin went.

"I know James," Wolfe said.

"He said that?" Miranda asked.

"Said what?"

"That he still intended to marry me?"

"Yes, he did."

"That's nonsense," Wolfe said. "Miranda would never marry James Martin. . . . Would you?"

"Shut up, Jeffery."

"Miranda—"

"So, he wouldn't admit that Flood was acting on his behalf?" she asked, ignoring Wolfe.

"He wouldn't discuss his business with me."

"*His* business," she said derisively. "His business is his father's business. It's James, Senior, who holds the purse strings."

"Martin, Jr., has no money of his own?"

"He has some, but every deal he makes he clears through his daddy."

"You don't like a man who works for his daddy?" Clint asked.

"Works for him? He worships the ground he walks on. He doesn't make a move without him. That's not a man, that's a . . . a puppet."

"Well," Clint said, "I guess I talked to the wrong Martin, didn't I?"

"If you like," Wolfe said, "I can probably get you in to see Mr. Martin . . . Senior, I mean."

"No, that's okay," Clint said, remembering the piece of paper in his pocket. "I have my own contacts."

When Clint was ready to leave, it was obvious that Wolfe wasn't.

"Jeffery," Miranda said, "why don't you help Clint get a cab."

"All right," Wolfe said, "I'll be back—"

"I'm really tired, Jeffery," she said. "Why don't we talk tomorrow."

"Well . . . okay," Wolfe said, "if that's the way you want it."

As Wolfe was getting his jacket on, Clint exchanged a glance with Miranda, and then a smile. They both knew how crushed Wolfe was at being put out, and they were sharing that behind his back.

SEVENTEEN

The next morning Clint was outside Brenda Loring's rooms when she came out to go to work.

"Hello," he said, stepping from the doorway next to hers.

She didn't exhibit any surprise at his appearance.

"Are you going to try to tell me this is a coincidence?" she asked.

"No," he said, "no coincidence at all."

"Well," she said, "when I gave you my address I didn't really expect you to show up so early. What can I do for you?"

"I'd like to talk to you."

"Just talk?"

He smiled and said, "For now."

"Well," she said, "I really don't have time to talk right now."

"Not even time for a cup of coffee?"

She shook her head.

"I'm on my way to work, and I don't want to be late.

Being late is not the way to keep a job, and I want to keep this job."

"Why?"

"Why?" she repeated. "Because it pays well, that's why."

"Are you walking to work?"

"Yes," she said, "it's good exercise. It keeps my thighs from getting too fat."

"Your thighs look fine to me."

"Hey," she said, "you're not shy, are you?"

"No. Why?"

"I'm tired of shy men," she said. She looked down at herself and said, "Maybe I'll give you a chance to see how fat my thighs are."

"Maybe I'll take you up on the offer," he said, "but first I want to talk."

"All right," she said, "walk with me for a while and we'll talk."

They started walking down the street.

"What can you tell me about your boss?"

"Are you talking about James, Junior?"

"Yes."

"James, Junior, is not my boss," she said. "James, Senior, is. Junior *thinks* he's my boss, but it's Senior who pays my salary."

"What does Junior do?"

"Well, he doesn't check out my thighs, if that's what you mean," she said. "I like men with a mind of their own, and Junior is about as far from that type as could be."

"What does that mean, exactly?"

"That he doesn't do anything without Daddy's okay," she said. "I think he even asks his father what color tie he should wear in the morning."

"How much do you know about the business of the Martins, Junior and Senior?"

"I know whatever they want me to know."

"How much of that will you tell me?"

"That depends."

"On what?"

"On how expensive a dinner you want to buy me tonight," she said. "And on what happens afterward."

"What could happen afterward?"

She eyed him and said, "I thought you weren't shy." She put her hand on his chest and said, "Come by tonight, at seven. We'll have dinner and talk some more."

"Aren't you afraid that talking to me about your boss's business will cost you your job?"

"They don't have to know," she said. "Besides, I never let business interfere with my private life. I'll see you tonight."

He watched as she walked down the street, a girl who was definitely not shy, who knew what she wanted and probably how to get it. He thought he knew what she wanted from him, and he wasn't going to be too disappointed if it turned out he was right.

EIGHTEEN

After talking with Brenda Loring on the run, Clint went to the police station to see McIntyre. Apparently Wolfe had left instructions that Clint was to be allowed to see his client but that no one else was.

McIntyre hadn't shaved in days and was starting to look like a grizzled old prospector. His gray hair was in disarray, and his beard was gray and white. Clint sniffed the air and determined that the older man also needed a bath.

"That young lawyer seems to be a go-getter," McIntyre said when Clint entered the cell. "Where did you manage to find him?"

"He was recommended by your partner."

"Miranda?"

Clint nodded.

"Apparently they're friends."

"Uh-oh."

"Uh-oh . . . what?"

"You and women."

"What are you talking about?"

"Miranda. You like her."

"So?"

"So that always leads to trouble," McIntyre said. "Don't go upsetting my young lawyer."

"Let me tell what your young lawyer has come up with, and we'll see who gets upset."

"What are you talking about?" McIntyre asked. "Didn't he get me my bail?"

"He wants you to stay in jail."

"What?" McIntyre jumped to his feet.

"Before you go off half-cocked, let me tell you what his thinking is."

Clint explained Wolfe's reasoning to McIntyre, who listened impatiently.

"That's crazy," McIntyre said when Clint was finished. "I'm not staying in here."

"Think about it calmly for a moment, John," Clint said. "If I have to guard you, I can't find out who really killed Flood."

"Nobody has to guard me," McIntyre said irritably. "I can take care of myself."

"Look," Clint said, "I hate to say it, but I agree with Wolfe. I think it would be better for everyone concerned if you stayed in this cell. I'll talk to Watson about getting you some decent meals."

"I ain't worried about meals," McIntyre said. "I want to get out of here and get my hands on the yahoo who's framing me."

"I'll take care of that, Mac, believe me," Clint said. "I need for you to be somewhere safe so I don't have to worry about you."

"What am I, your goddamned father?" McIntyre demanded.

"No," Clint said, "you're my friend, John, and I want to keep you alive."

"Damn you, Adams," McIntyre said, flopping down on the cot.

"You'll do it? You'll stay?"

"I'll stay," McIntyre said reluctantly, "for a while, but you better show me some results, boy."

"I've got some results, John," Clint said, and told McIntyre about the Martins, Junior and Senior.

"So Flood was a flunky, huh?" McIntyre asked. "He wasn't the big shot he made himself out to be. I like that a lot."

"I thought you might."

"But who had reason to kill him?"

"That's what I have to find out," Clint said. "I assume he was a tough boss, which means it could have been one of the people who work for him."

"Or one of the people he works for."

"That's what I have to find out," Clint said. "I've talked to Martin, Junior, but I went in unprepared. I intend to talk to his father, but I've got some preparations to make first."

"What kind?"

"I've got a dinner date with his secretary tonight," Clint said. "I think I can get her to talk to me."

"Uh-oh."

"Uh-oh, what?"

"Uh-oh, you and women . . ."

Clint took a deep breath, let it out, and said, "Don't start that again."

"I can't help it," McIntyre said. "I never saw a man who attracted women like honey attracts flies. What is it about you, son?"

"I guess I know how to treat them, John," Clint said.

"That's what I like the most about you, Clint," McIntyre said.

"What?"

"Your modesty."

Clint walked to the cell door and called out for the guard. He turned to face McIntyre.

"I'll talk to Watson about some food."

"Steak," McIntyre said. "I need steak."

"I'll try."

"Maybe you can get Miranda to cook something and send it over," McIntyre said. "She does cook, doesn't she?"

The guard opened the door, and before going through it Clint said, "She cooks . . . after a fashion."

NINETEEN

Clint used the rest of the day to get someone to go out and haul the damaged coach back to the Gold Stage Line stable. He also hired some men to go out and search for the six-horse team. They were probably out wandering the area. Since murder was involved, he doubted that the men involved would want to take a chance of being caught trying to sell the horses.

All that done, he went to the office to wait, and found Miranda at the desk.

"Hi," she said, smiling.

"Hello," he said. "I want to thank you again for dinner last night."

"Oh, that's all right," she said. "I'm sorry about Jeffery. He can be . . . overbearing at times."

"I know."

She laughed and said, "You know what's funny? He doesn't even know it. It just comes natural to him."

"I assume that he has had dinner at your house quite a few times."

"That's what he'd like you to think," she said. "Actually, last night was only the second time."

"He must be in love with you," Clint said. "He kept posting warning signs."

"I suppose he is," she said. "He's nice enough, and he's a good attorney, but he's also several years younger than I am."

"What are you doing here?" he asked.

She looked down at the desk and said, "Catching up on some paperwork. I also sent a telegram to our Rock Springs station. That's between here and San Francisco. They've got four horses there that we can use. I have to let them know if I want them brought here or not."

"Let's hold off on that for a while."

"Why?"

He explained his activities of the morning, and suggested they wait to see if any of the horses were brought back.

"The coach should be here soon."

"Where did you get the money for this?"

"Don't worry about the money."

"But . . . the line will pay you back."

"I'll get it from McIntyre. Don't worry."

She studied him for a moment, then said, "No, you won't. You won't ask him for the money, will you?"

He hesitated a moment, then said, "No."

"Why not?"

"Because he's my friend."

"Well then, I'll pay you back."

"No," he said, "you won't."

"Why not?"

He walked up to her and put his hands on her waist.

"Because you're my friend, too."

"Wha——" she said, but he pulled her to him and kissed her. She didn't react at first. She didn't resist, but she didn't help, either. He slid his hands to her back and pulled her close to him, kissing her with increased ardor. Finally she slid her arms behind him and pressed herself to him, answering the insistent pressure of his lips and tongue with her own.

Breaking the kiss, he asked, "What's in the back room here?"

Breathlessly she said, "It's a bedroom. There's a bed back there."

He took her hand and walked her to the door. She resisted when they reached it. He pulled on her hand then, and this was the test. If she still resisted, he would have stopped, but she came to him when he pulled and allowed him to lead her into the back room.

He unbuttoned her blouse first and removed it. He removed her undergarment then, and her breasts flowed into his hands. He caressed her breasts for a few moments, popping the nipples between his thumb and forefinger. She moaned and closed her eyes, leaning into him.

He got down on his knees next and reached under her skirt. He helped remove her skirt and then her shoes so he could finally press his face to the warm skin of her belly. Her kissed her navel, sliding his hands around to cup her buttocks, which were firm and muscular. He kneaded them, peppering her belly with kisses, and then lowered his head to lick the slit between her legs. She groaned and moved her legs, giving him better access, and he made her wet by licking her avidly. She put her hands on his shoulders and leaned on him while he probed her with his tongue, and then she shuddered and her legs shook.

He stood up and led her to the bed, letting her lie on her back. He removed his clothes, and she watched him, licking her lips. Her chest was heaving, the nipples of her breasts hard and tight.

He moved to the side of the bed and stood there. She stared at his erect penis, then reached out and touched it, tentatively at first, and then closing her hand around it tightly.

He got on the bed with her, lying next to her, and began to kiss her neck, her shoulder, and her breasts. She cupped his head, wrapping her hands in his hair as he nuzzled her nipples.

"Jesus," she said, the first word spoken by either of them in minutes.

He slid one thigh over her, then the other, and lifted himself above her, one hand on either side of her. She reached between them to fondle his penis, then put her hands on his hips and pulled him to her. She spread her legs, and he slid into her easily. She closed her eyes, arched her neck, and moaned.

He moved in her slowly at first, and then more urgently. He kissed her, probing her mouth with his tongue while he fucked her, and her arms came around him convulsively. She scraped his back with her nails as his tempo increased, and then her hands fell to her sides as she grabbed tight handfuls of the sheet.

He slid one hand beneath, supporting her lower back, and pulled her to him as she climaxed again. He started moving in her faster now, until finally he groaned and exploded into her. . . .

They dressed afterward, in silence, and he wondered if he had gone too fast, done the wrong thing. When they were both dressed she turned to him, her hands clasped in front of her primly.

"Well," she said, "I guess that does classify us as friends, doesn't it?"

He felt relief flood through him.

"I guess so."

Before either of them could say anything else, they heard a wagon outside. They both flicked their eyes toward the front office, but neither seemed willing to move just yet.

"Maybe those are the men bringing the coach back," he said, finally.

"We'd better check the damage and see if it can be salvaged."

"Yes," he said, "we'd better."

They stared at each other for a few seconds, and then she moved first, and he followed her out.

Clint was a little surprised at himself, and at how quickly it had happened. He really had had no intention of . . . of seducing her . . . certainly not right there in the office. Not that he hadn't thought about her in bed with him, but he would have thought that it would take place in her house, or his hotel, or after they at least had spent some more time alone together.

As they stepped outside, he couldn't help wondering if James Martin, Junior, or Jeffery Wolfe had ever been to bed with her.

TWENTY

They had the men place the coach inside the stable, and then Clint paid them out of his pocket. Miranda started to argue with him again about the money, but he cut her off.

"Friends don't argue about money," he said.

She frowned. She didn't seem convinced, but apparently decided to leave the discussion for the moment.

"The coach doesn't look too bad," she said.

Indeed, all the men had to do was get it right side up, and then they hitched it to the back of their wagon and pulled it into Sacramento.

"Some bullet holes," she said, looking it over, "some . . . blood. . . ."

He heard the catch in her throat and said, "I'll look inside."

He climbed inside and looked around. A bucket of water and some rags and the blood would wash away. The vision of the boy's arm sticking out from underneath the coach, however—that would be with him for a while.

"Clint?"

He started, realizing that she had called his name several times.

"Huh? Sorry."

She was looking in the window from the other side of the coach.

"Maybe I should have checked the inside."

"No, it's all right," he said. "I was just thinking . . . about the boy. He . . . was pinned underneath the coach when it fell. The first thing I saw was . . . his arm sticking out from underneath."

She reached into the coach to comfort him, but couldn't reach him.

"I'm sorry you found him."

He looked at her and said, "The men who killed him are going to be sorry when I find *them*."

He backed out of the coach and closed the door harder than necessary. It stood the pounding, which was good to know.

"Well," he said, "a good wash and some patching of the bullet holes, and she'll be as good as new."

"We were reduced to two runs a week," she said. "The next one is Friday." This was Wednesday. "If we had a team—and a driver—we could make it."

"The team may not be so hard," Clint said, "but getting a driver to drive for you, after what happened . . ."

"Couldn't you drive?" she asked.

"Miranda, I can't—"

"I'm sorry," she said, raising one hand to ward off his refusal. "I had no right to ask—"

"No," he said, "you don't understand. Let me finish. I'm not experienced with a six-horse team. I'm just not qualified for this kind of driving job. If we can get a driver, though, I'll be glad to ride shotgun."

"I'm sorry," she said. "Yes, that would be fine."

"In fact," he said, "maybe we could get someone else to ride along, also. As extra backup, I mean."

"Who?"

"I don't know yet," he said. "Let's take one step at a time."

"And step one is?"

"Getting a team," he said. "We'll give the other men I hired time to bring the team back."

"And if they don't?"

"And then maybe we'll have to send for the Rock Springs team."

"That will only be four," she said. "We'd still need two more."

"We could get them . . . somewhere. Look, are you hungry? 'Cause I am."

"Yes," she said, "I am hungry."

"Let's go and get an early dinner. Maybe one of us will come up with a brilliant idea."

"I have to warn you," she said, "I'm not a great idea person."

"Don't worry," he said, taking her arm, "we'll think of something together."

Carp was very excited. He had passed the word that he wanted to see James Martin, Senior, and now he had gotten the word to come and see—and not at his office, but at his Cobblestone home. Cobblestone was a section of the city where only the very rich lived. Carp felt terribly out of place as he approached the front door and knocked.

A butler answered the door, looked him up and down, and then said haughtily, "Yes?"

"I have an appointment to see Mr. Martin."

"Junior or Senior?" the butler asked.

Carp straightened his back and said, "Senior, of course."

"Of course," the butler said. "Your name?"

"Carp."

"Yes," the butler said. "Please come in."

This was the first time in his life that Carp felt as if his name were a magic word.

TWENTY-ONE

Over dinner Clint came up with one idea.

"The marshal."

"Does he know how to drive a team?" Miranda asked.

"He drove a team for years before he started upholding the law."

"Wasn't that a long time ago?" she asked.

"Maybe, but I don't think he's forgotten. You know, I'll bet that's why he accepted your father's part of the business in the poker game."

She nodded.

"What about what Jeffery said?"

"I still agree with what good ol' Jeff said," Clint said, "but we need a driver, and where else do we have to turn? Uh, Jeff can't drive a team, can he?"

She gave him a look that was all the answer they needed, and they both laughed.

"There is one other option."

"What?" he asked.

"Me?"

"You can drive a team?"

"My father taught me when I was young. I haven't driven one in years, but like you said—"

"No," Clint said, "we need you in the office."

"To do what?" she demanded.

"To stay out of harm's way."

"That's not fair," she said. "This company is mine, not yours. Why should you take the risks?"

"Because it's what I know how to do," Clint said. "John called me here to help, and that's what I'm going to do— but first I've got to get him out of jail."

"You ought to make up your damn mind!" McIntyre said as he and Clint left the police station.

"Look," Clint said, "I only got you out to keep your business alive. You need a driver for your next run."

"Me?" he said. "I haven't driven a team in years."

"So what? You still know how, don't you?"

"Well . . . probably, but we don't have a team."

"One problem at a time," Clint said. "So far we have a driver and a shotgun."

"You."

"Right."

"What's next?"

"A team," Clint said. He explained that he had men out looking for the original team, and told him about the four horses at Rock Springs.

"Even if we get our team back," McIntyre said, "we should still get the horses from Rock Springs."

"Why?"

"To keep an eye on them," McIntyre said. "If someone wants to put us out of business, it makes sense they'd try for those horses."

Clint gave the older man an admiring look and said, "That's why you were always the marshal and I was always the deputy."

"Don't forget about Coronado."

"Coronado?"

"You were the marshal and I was the deputy."

Clint remembered. He had been hired as marshal in the Arizona Territory, with his office in Coronado. He needed help, and sent a telegram to McIntyre, who came running. Together, they cleaned up Coronado.

"One time."

"That was the last time we worked together," McIntyre said, "before this."

"That's right," Clint said thoughtfully, "it was. How long ago was that?"

"Eight years."

"It's been eight years since we saw each other last?" Clint asked.

"At least. But who's counting?"

"You know," Clint said, "with everything that's been happening, we haven't gotten a chance to catch up. What have you been doing for the past eight years?"

"Well," McIntyre said, "for the past two years I've sort of been the town drunk of Sacramento."

TWENTY-TWO

As enigmatic as the remark was, they didn't have time for McIntyre to explain it. When they got back to the office, Miranda was out front holding three horses. There were two men there with her.

"These men said you promised them ten dollars a head," she said.

"That I did," Clint said. He took out the money and gave it to them. "Keep looking, huh?"

"It's gettin' late," one of the men said.

"I'll make it twenty a head."

The man smiled and said, "We'll keep looking."

As they rode off and Miranda led the horses into the stable, McIntyre said to Clint, "Where are you getting the money to pay them to round up our horses?"

"Don't worry about that."

"Clint," McIntyre said, "I didn't ask you to come here to hit you for money—"

"You asked me to come and help," Clint said, "and I'm helping."

"Well, this isn't exactly what I had in mind."

"What *did* you have in mind for me, John?"

McIntyre hesitated and then said, "I don't know, Clint. I really don't know. Let's go inside."

Clint felt he should go in the stable and help Miranda with the horses, but he followed McIntyre into the office. He found his friend rooting around in the desk.

"Where the hell did I put it?"

"What are you looking for?"

"A bottle of whiskey I had in here," McIntyre said. He slammed the bottom drawer closed and straightened up. "Oh, yeah, now I remember."

"What?"

"I threw it over there," McIntyre said, indicating a corner of the room. There was nothing there now, since Miranda had been cleaning up.

"John, what you said before about being the town drunk . . ."

"I fell on hard times," McIntyre said, "and fell right into a bottle."

"For two years?"

"No, I fell in pretty quick, but it took me two years to climb out."

"And when you did, you won this place from Miranda's father in a poker game?"

"That was funny," McIntyre said, sitting behind the desk. "You know, I was sober a week when I got into that card game. Boy, did I get hot. I was pulling cards out of the air, Clint. You shoulda seen me."

"John," Clint said warily, "you weren't cheating, were you?"

"Hell, no," McIntyre said. "My hands were shaking too

much for me to be cheating. I told you, I'd only been sober a week."

At that point Miranda opened the door and walked in. She stopped when she saw them.

"I'm sorry," she said. "Did I interrupt something?"

"No, Miranda," Clint said, "we were just catching up. How are the horses?"

"A little played out, but they've got a full day to rest. We're going to need three more, though."

"We'll get them."

"Hey," McIntyre said, because he'd just noticed, "you cleaned up in here."

"Big difference, huh?" she asked. "I meant to ask you, Mr. McIntyre, did you break a bottle and spill something in that corner?" She pointed to the corner into which he had thrown the whiskey bottle.

"Uh, yes, Miranda, I did," McIntyre said. "I'm sorry I didn't have a chance to clean it up."

"That's all right," she said. "Now that I've finished in here, I'm going to have to clean the back room."

"Hey, that would be great," McIntyre said, "since that's where I'm going to be sleeping. I can't afford to stay in a hotel forever."

Clint and Miranda exchanged a glance and a smile, like two people who were sharing a private joke.

TWENTY-THREE

James Martin, Senior, kept Carp waiting, but Carp didn't mind. Just the fact that he was going to see the man made him start to think about living better. If he could get James Martin, Senior's, confidence . . .

"Mr. Martin will see you now," the butler finally said. "This way, please."

Carp got up and followed the butler down a long hallway to an office. The butler opened the door and stepped aside. Carp, his heart pounding, stepped into the room.

"Sit down, Mr. Carp," Martin commanded.

James Martin, Senior, had a commanding presence. Not only was he tall—six-foot-four—but also he was barrel-chested and heavily bearded. In one way or another he dwarfed and intimidated most men.

Carp sat down.

"I understand you worked closely with Mr. Flood."

"That's right . . . sir."

"You passed the word that you wanted to see me about Mr. Flood."

"That's right, sir."

"What was it you wanted to tell me?"

Carp told Martin about a man asking a lot of questions about Flood and how he was killed.

"Who was the man?"

"I asked around," Carp said. He knew Martin was going to ask this question, and he wanted to have the answer. "His name is Clint Adams. He's a friend of that old marshal, McIntyre. He owns the Gold Stage Line."

"I am aware of who owns the Gold Stage Line, Mr. Carp," Martin said.

"Sorry," Carp said, feeling chastised.

Martin sat and stroked his beard.

"Is this Clint Adams the same man who is known as the Gunsmith?"

"I . . . guess so," Carp said uncertainly.

"Yes, of course he is," Martin said. "All right, Mr. Carp. I may be calling on you in the near future. Will you be available?"

"Yes, sir," Carp said immediately.

"Very good," Martin said. "My butler will see you out, and he will have something for you."

"Yes, sir," Carp said, standing up. "Thank you."

Carp turned and left the room and found the butler waiting for him in the hall. Wordlessly, the man led him to the front door, handed him an envelope, and saw him out. On the front steps Carp opened the envelope and saw that it was filled—*filled*—with money.

And this was just the beginning, Carp knew.

Yep, the quality of his life was definitely going to improve.

• • •

After Carp was shown out, James Martin, Senior, sat back in his chair and thought about Clint Adams. First he was at the saloon asking about Flood's death, and then he was right in the office, talking to the younger James. Martin frowned. He was aware that his son and Flood had a relationship, but he didn't know the full extent of it. He also didn't know whether the boy had anything to do with Flood's death. On one hand, if he did, at least it would show that his son was at last showing some initiative and backbone. On the other hand, if he was involved in murder, the elder Martin was going to have to do his best to keep the boy out of jail. Of course, if he was going to keep his son out of jail, that meant that someone else would have to take his place. Carp might even be a good choice for that.

As for Adams, if this was the same man they called the Gunsmith, there wasn't anyone in Sacramento who was qualified to deal with him.

It was obviously time to bring in some out-of-town talent, and when James Martin, Senior, did that, it was usually high-priced talent.

TWENTY-FOUR

Clint, McIntyre, and Miranda were sitting around the office that evening, for want of anything better to do, when they heard someone ride up outside. Clint checked and found that the two men had brought back one more horse. He paid them, and then he and Miranda walked the animal into the stable.

"Oh, damn!" Clint said.

"What?"

"I didn't check on my horse today," Clint said. "He probably thinks I abandoned him."

"Your horse thinks that?" she said, staring at him.

Clint smiled and said, "He's a very smart horse. I'll have to make sure I check on him in the morning."

"What was wrong with him?"

"He picked up a stone bruise on the way in," Clint said. "That was what caused me to hitch a ride on the coach."

"Why don't you bring him here?" she suggested.

"That's a good idea," Clint said. "In fact, I think I should

111

move in here with the marshal."

"To keep an eye on him?"

"To keep an eye on everything," Clint said. "Him, the horses, the coach, the place. I want to make sure everything is in shape for the run on Friday."

"Good thinking."

"On the way back we'll pick up the other horses from Rock Springs." He explained McIntyre's reasoning for bringing the horses to Sacramento.

"Do you really think they'll try to steal the horses?" she asked.

"Or kill them," Clint said. "After what happened to the people in the coach, anything's possible."

"What could be worse than that?"

"I hope we don't have to find out. Uh, Miranda, I have to leave for a while."

"Oh?"

"Yes, I have an appointment for dinner with someone who might tell me something I need to know about James Martin, Senior."

"Like what?"

"Like if he had any interest in buying you out," Clint said. "I'd like to find out once and for all whether Flood was working for himself, or for the Martins."

"I'd prefer that the Martins weren't behind him," she said.

"Why?"

"I'd just prefer not to have any dealings with them," she said. "It's been a while since I saw either one of them, and I'd like to keep it that way."

He smiled at her and said, "I'll do my best. Why don't you go inside and talk to McIntyre? See if you can keep him indoors until I get back."

"That may be tough if he gets hungry."

"When I get back I'll buy you both a late dinner."

"You'll already have had dinner."

He grinned at her and said, "I'll eat light."

By the time Clint presented himself at Brenda Loring's room, it was getting dark. She opened the door and smiled beautifully at him.

"Well, you're right on time," she said. "I like a man to be prompt."

"Are you hungry?"

"I'm famished."

"I'll have to leave the choice of restaurant to you," he said. "I didn't exactly have anything fancy to put on."

"Don't worry about that," she said. "I'm simply dressed." She was, but her body had a way of making a simple dress look special. "I like to eat in a place with good food, not fancy atmosphere."

"I feel the same way."

"Well then," she said, sliding her arm through his, "come along. I think you'll approve of my choice."

TWENTY-FIVE

Clint did, indeed, approve of Brenda's choice of restaurant. There was sawdust on the floor, and most of the dishes consisted of some sort of meat and potatoes. "Simple eating" the sign outside the restaurant promised, and that's what it delivered.

"Men like Mr. Martin," she said, when they each had a steak in front of them, "they take their clients to places that serve French food, or creole food, or something else fancy like that, but I like to eat plain old meat and potatoes. That's why I'm always a good fifteen to twenty pounds overweight."

"I wouldn't say you were overweight," Clint said.

"What would you say I was?" she asked.

"Just fine."

"Just fine," Brenda said, "for a chubby girl. No, it's all right," she said, warding off any more of his denials about her figure. "I could lose twenty pounds, but then I feel too skinny. I think I like myself better this way, with some meat on my bones."

"I like women with meat on their bones."

"Well, good," she said. "Now that we've got that settled, why don't you ask me what you want to ask me."

"Brenda—"

"No, no," she said, reaching across to put one of her hands over his, "let's get the business out of the way, Clint."

"All right," he said, "but you don't mind if I continue to eat while we talk, do you? This is really good."

"No, go right ahead," she said. "That's just what I intend to do."

"Let's go over what you told me already," Clint said. "What are James, Junior, and James, Senior, like?"

"Let's put it this way," she said. "They are totally different from each other. There is not one way in which they are similar, except one."

"What way is that?"

"Women," she said. "They both love women."

"Are they married?"

"No," she said. "Senior's wife died years ago, and Junior never married."

"How senior is Senior?"

"He's fifty-eight, but he's got the constitution of a bull. He escorts women half his age to the ballet and the opera."

"And then takes them home?"

"Yes," she said, "home with him."

"You mean at his age he's still—"

"Very virile."

"Do you know from firsthand experience," he asked, "or am I getting too personal?"

"I've never been to bed with either of them," she said, "but I'll tell you this: If Junior asked me, I'd say no."

"And if Senior asked?"

She put both hands beneath her chin and stared at him.

"I'd say I'd have to consider it," she said. "Even if

it was just to ease my curiosity."

"Do you think maybe he takes those young women home with them and sleeps in a separate room? Maybe he pays them not to tell?"

"No," she said, "I know two women personally who he took home with him. They say he's like a bull that's always in heat."

"Well," Clint said, "I suppose I should be impressed."

"What about you, Clint?" she asked. She still had her fists beneath her chin.

"What about me?"

"Are you like a bull in heat?"

"I thought we were going to get the business out of the way first."

"Oh, all right." She picked up her fork and speared a piece of meat from her plate.

"What about their business practices?"

"What about them?"

"Are they involved in anything . . . borderline illegal?"

"Not Senior."

"Are you sure?"

"Positive," she said. "He's a stickler for staying within the law . . . when it comes to business."

"Why did you qualify that statement?"

"Because," she said, "he's bent the law many times to keep his sons and daughter out of trouble."

"He has other children?"

"Altogether," she said, "he has two sons and one daughter. One son is a lawyer in San Francisco. That's Brent, the oldest. He was a hellion in his early days, but he finally grew up and met his father's expectations."

"Which James, Junior, has not?"

"James, Junior, for some reason, is the apple of his father's eye, but he's a terrible disappointment to James, Senior."

"Why?"

"He has very little personal courage. Even when he was tomcatting around, getting into trouble in the gambling halls when he was younger, he always relied on his father's name and reputation to get him out of trouble. It even kept him out of fights, which was good because James is not a fighter."

"And has he stopped tomcatting around and getting into trouble?"

"When he turned thirty his father put his foot down. He told James, Junior, that either he came into the business and stopped fooling around, or he would disinherit him."

"Did it work?"

"Like a bucket of cold water. For the past four years James, Junior, has been the soul of discretion with his women and his gambling."

"But he's stopped neither."

"Oh, no," she said, "he wouldn't stop, but he does both in private, now."

"What about business? What kind does Junior do?"

"Whatever Senior gives him to do," she said, "which isn't much. James, Junior, has no business sense at all, and more often than not Senior has to step in and rescue deals from his son's ineptness."

"What about his dealings with Flood? Did Senior know about that?"

"He knew that James knew Flood. Senior thought that was good. Flood was more the way Senior wanted Junior to be, and he thought some of it might rub off. He let Junior go into business with Flood."

"Like the saloon?"

"Yes."

"What about the stage line?"

"What about it?"

"Who wanted to buy that? Senior or Junior?"

She shook her head.

"I don't know anything about either of them wanting to buy a stage line," she said. "It never crossed my desk."

"What if Junior was interested, and had Flood fronting for him? Would he want Senior to know?"

"If he was doing something on his own? No, he wouldn't want his father to know unless the deal went through and was a success. James very much wants his father to be proud of him, but he just doesn't have the business sense to pull it off."

"Maybe he was leaving that part of Flood."

"Maybe."

"Did you know Flood?"

"I met him once or twice," she answered, averting her eyes, "when he came to see Junior."

Clint didn't quite believe her, but he didn't push it. Maybe she knew Flood better than she wanted Clint to know, but he didn't particularly care if she had slept with Flood or not.

As it turned out, she knew very little that would help Clint in trying to figure out who had killed Flood. Senior knew Flood, and hoped he would make a man of Junior. No motive there. Junior knew Flood and used him as a front man. Where was the motive there, unless they had a falling out over business?

The only way he'd find out anything about that is if he got Brenda to admit she knew Flood better. Maybe, if she had slept with Flood, he might have let something slip.

He didn't want to approach that subject in the restaurant, but after dinner, when she proposed that they go back to her rooms, he readily accepted.

He was fully prepared to do what it took to get the information out of her.

TWENTY-SIX

Brenda Loring nude was a breathtaking sight. That extra fifteen or twenty pounds that she carried around turned to be extremely firm, rather than fat. Her breasts were very large, but round and firm. Standing there staring at her, he was put in mind of two cannonballs—even more so when she turned to walk to the bed, showing him her big, firm butt.

She turned down the bed, moving in her nudity with extreme confidence. Although she talked about herself being fat, she knew that the extra poundage only added to her allure for any man who liked big women.

"Your turn, darling," Brenda said to him after having turned down the bed. "Undress."

He took a moment longer to stare at her. Her nipples were dark brown and tight, the flesh of her breasts as smooth as glass. Her hips were wide, her thighs fleshy as she stood with her legs spread, her hands on her hips, waiting.

Finally he started undressing, removing his shirt, pulling off his boots, then dropping his pants and kicking them away.

"Wait," she said, moving toward him, "let me finish the job."

She got on her knees in front of him and grasped the waist of his shorts. She tugged them down slowly, inch by inch, until just the swollen head of his penis showed.

"Umm," she said, leaning over to run her tongue over him. Slowly still, she pulled the shorts down, until his penis was standing erect in front of her. She eased the shorts down his legs so he could step out of them, then pressed her breasts against his thighs, rubbing her nipples over him, pressing his penis to the cleft between her full breasts. She had almost no cleavage because her breasts were so full they pressed against one another.

She pressed her face against his stomach, running her tongue over him, running her hands behind him, moving her palms over his buttocks. Suddenly she clutched at his buttocks, licked her lips, and brought her mouth down on his penis, engulfing it. She began to suck him noisily, moaning in appreciation, her nails digging into the flesh of his ass. He reached down and took her head in his hands, just holding her while her head bounced up and down, her lips and teeth doing wild things to his penis, which was glistening from her saliva.

Finally, Clint had more than he could handle and he tried to pull free of her mouth. She was reluctant to release him, but finally allowed him to slide free.

He pulled her to her feet and greedily filled his hands with her breasts.

"Jesus," he said, "you're so firm . . ."

"Fat, you mean," she said, breathing hard. "You must like fat women, Clint Adams."

Abruptly, he pushed her away from him so hard that she fell onto the bed.

"What . . ." she said, her eyes widening.

"You can stop the bullshit, Brenda," he said. "You know you have a body that most men would kill for. Full and firm, healthy and . . . and sexy . . ."

"Ooh, keep talking . . ."

"No," he said, "I don't think I will."

He leaned over her and ran his mouth over her cannonball breasts. He licked the smooth flesh, bit the hard nipples, and while doing so ran his hand over her belly, her thighs, finally sliding it between her legs, where she was wet and sticky.

"Oh," she said, wiggling her butt, "ooh, yes . . ."

He dipped first one finger into her, then another, still crouched over her, still kissing and licking her breasts. The odor of her sweat and her sex was acting like some sort of aphrodisiac on him. His heart was pounding, and his penis was as hard as a column of steel.

Suddenly he fell to his knees and pulled her to the end of the bed, so that her legs were hanging over the edge. He ran his mouth over her belly, her thighs, and then used his tongue on the dark, wiry patch of hair between her legs until he broke through and tasted her.

His penis was so hard that it was difficult for him to believe that he had just that afternoon had sex with Miranda Ross. He felt as if he had not had a woman in months. He was a man coming off of a desert, and Brenda Loring was an oasis.

He braced his elbows on her powerful thighs and went to work on her with his mouth and tongue. Brenda Loring gasped and tried to squirm, but he had her pinned to the bed.

"Oh, God . . ." she gasped as he tongued her, "oh, Jesus, you have to . . . let me . . . move . . . oh, oooh . . ."

He found her stiff little clit and latched on to it, sucking it, flicking at it with his tongue, and she erupted beneath him, grabbing for him with her hands and pulling at him until he had crawled atop her. He lifted his hips just long enough to position the head of his penis against the slick lips of her pussy, and then she grabbed his buttocks and drove him inside of her. She lifted her powerful legs and wrapped them around him. He could feel her hard breasts beneath his chest, refusing to be crushed by his weight, her nipples digging into him like hard pebbles. He slid his hands beneath her, cupped her chunky buttocks, and began to drive into her like a man possessed only with his own pleasure. The way she was moaning and crying out beneath him, clutching at him with powerful arms and legs, it was clear that she was deriving as much pleasure from their coupling as he was.

He felt the great rush building up inside of him and wasn't sure he could hold back the torrent that was threatening to burst free when suddenly she shouted, "Oh, yes, it's . . . it's here . . . it's here!"

He exploded inside of her, and they were both there together. . . .

Later they lay among the damp, wrinkled sheets, side by side, trying to catch their breath.

"When you walked into the office," she said breathlessly, "I knew then that we were going to be together . . . but I never expected anything like . . . like that!"

To be frank with himself, he had never expected anything like that, either. He had recognized her as a woman who knew what she wanted, and he was even flattered that she wanted him. She was certainly a desirable woman, and he knew it would be no hardship to go to bed with her. He fully intended to enjoy himself when he did, but he never expected to be so excited by her firm, muscular body that he would almost completely lose control!

"Jesus," she said, running her hands over her sweating body, "I'm still tingling. You . . . you were . . . I thought you were . . . going to fuck me . . . to death."

He laughed.

"No chance of that happening, Brenda," he said. "I don't think there's a man alive who could do that."

"Oh, I do," she said, and now she ran her hands over his sweaty body. "I never thought I would ever find a man who could . . . could satisfy me . . . who could keep up with me."

"You are an incredibly sensual woman, Brenda."

"I know that," she said, immodestly. "I love sex, Clint, but I . . . I never had it . . . like . . . like this with you. . . ."

Clint knew that the same words had been spoken by many women over the years, some of them whores praising their johns as part of the package, but he thought he knew when a woman meant it, and Brenda Loring meant it.

"Brenda—"

"Oh, no," she said, "don't tell me you're going to leave, Clint Adams."

She rolled over so that she was lying atop him, her hands on his shoulders.

"I'm not through with you yet!"

She leaned over him so that her solid breasts were inches from his face, and he began to lick them. He slid his hands down her spine until he was cupping her buttocks, and she arched her back, keeping her breasts in contact with his mouth, and pressing her groin down against his, pinning his erection between them.

He wondered, if and when she did finish with him, if he would be good for anything else in the near future.

TWENTY-SEVEN

Leaving Brenda Loring's rooms, Clint realized that he really didn't get much from her in the way of information beyond the fact that James, Junior, didn't dare make a move without checking first with James, Senior.

He found a cab on one of the empty, late-night Sacramento streets and thought it over on the way back to his hotel. Either James, Senior, was behind what was going on, or James, Junior, had finally decided to try to do something on his own. Maybe he felt that if he took Miranda's stage line away from her she would rush into his arms. Clint did not think that was the case.

Tomorrow, he and McIntyre would take the stage on its run from Sacramento to Rock Springs to San Francisco and back. Clint felt that sometime during the run, the answers to all their questions would become clear.

On a lighter note, he was sort of glad that he would be leaving Sacramento on the stage for a while. He had found himself involved with two strong women, intrigued by Miranda Ross's determination and beauty, and mesmerized by Brenda Loring's amazing body. The last thing he needed now was to get caught between them.

Carp was surprised to be summoned to a meeting with James Martin, Junior, at the Lucky Deuce. Carp entered the saloon and nodded to Vance, the bartender. The man behind the bar used his eyes to indicate the office, where Martin was obviously waiting for him.

Carp walked to the office door and knocked.

"Come!" Martin called.

Carp entered. The younger Martin was seated behind the desk.

"Come in, Carp," Martin said. "Close the door."

Carp obeyed, closing the door and approaching the desk.

"Sit down."

Carp sat.

"I understand you saw my father."

"Uh," Carp said. He was almost as intimidated by James Martin, Junior, as he had been by the man's father. Actually, he was intimidated by their money.

"What did you tell him?"

"He wanted to know about Clint Adams."

"What about him?"

"Just who he was, what he wanted."

"I see," Martin said. "Have you found out anything else about Clint Adams?"

"I sure have," Carp said. "He's going to make a run with the Gold Stage Line tomorrow."

"How?" Martin asked. "He's got no team, no coach, and no driver."

"Wrong," Carp said. "The old marshal, McIntyre, is gonna drive the coach, and they recovered four of their horses. All they have to do is get two more horses from the livery."

"They have no credit."

"They don't need it," Carp said. "Adams has cash."

"What about the coach?"

"They patched it up."

"Where did you hear all of this, Carp?"

"From one of the men who was hired to go out and look for the horses. He says he thinks they'll make their run tomorrow."

"To where?"

"San Francisco, by way of Rock Springs."

Martin rubbed his jaw, digesting all of the information he'd just gotten.

Slowly, he took out his wallet and started counting out bills on the desk.

"Carp," he said, not looking at the man but continuing to count out money, "I don't want that coach to make it to San Francisco. Do you understand?"

"Sure, Mr. Martin," Carp said, greedily eyeing the money on the desk, "I understand."

Martin started to put away his wallet, then changed his mind, opened it, and counted out a few more bills. That done, he pushed the bills across the smooth desktop to Carp's side.

"In fact," Martin said, "I don't want it to make it past Rock Springs."

"I understand, Mr. Martin," Carp said, picking up the money. "I'll take care of it."

As Carp stood up and walked toward the door, Martin said, "Carp."

"Yes, sir?"

"Nothing happens to the woman, understand? Don't touch Miranda Ross."

"Sure, Mr. Martin."

"And don't go to my father with this," Martin said,

"or I'll hire someone to kill you."

After a moment, Carp said softly, "Don't worry, Mr. Martin. I'm working for you."

"Remember that."

Carp left the room and entered the saloon. He looked around, then walked to the bar.

"Steve, have you seen Gates?"

"A while ago," Vance said. "He bought a bottle and said he was gonna go and share it with a whore."

"I know where to find him, then," Carp said. "Thanks."

"What's goin' on, Carp?"

"Oh," Carp said, "just business as usual."

Janey had the biggest tits of any of Millie's girls. That was why Gates liked her. It didn't matter to him that Janey was more than ten years older than he. All that mattered to him was that she sit astride him with his dick buried inside of her, letting him suck away at her strawberry nipples. He held the whiskey bottle in his left hand and alternated between sucking on it and on her big tits.

"You sure like my tits, Gates," Janey said. "Fact is, I don't think I ever been with a man who paid as much attention to them as you do. Most of the men hereabouts just want to stick their dick in me and get done with it." She wiggled on him, pushing herself down on him. His dick did things to her insides when she did that.

Blond, thirty-five, a whore since she was fifteen, Janey was one of those girls who admitted that, with some johns, she actually enjoyed sex. Gates was one of those because he was able to stay hard longer than any man she had ever known. That, and the amount of attention he lavished on her breasts made him special to her.

Also, he didn't talk much when they fucked—and she thought that it was probably time they started doing just that.

She leaned forward so that her pear-shaped breasts were dangling in front of her face, and started riding his rigid dick up and down. The movement caused her tits to sway and slap against each other, and he stared at them as if he were hypnotized.

"Oooh," she said, lifting her hips and ass higher and then coming down hard on him.

At that moment the door opened and Carp walked in.

"Carp," Gates said, frowning.

"Time to go, Gates," Carp said. "We have things to do."

"What kind of things?" Gates asked.

"The kind of things that pay very well."

"You don't have to tell me twice."

He lifted Janey off of him and tossed her aside.

"Hey!" she squealed.

"Take it easy, Janey," Carp said, eyeing her big, pale breasts. "He'll be back—or one of us will."

Janey shuddered, because she didn't like Carp a bit.

Carp watched as Gates got up and got dressed, struck once again by the size of his friend's penis. Gates was hung like a horse, and Carp had no idea what it must be like to carry something that monstrous around in your pants all day.

"Hey!" Janey called as both men headed for the door.

"You forgot to pay her," Carp said.

"Shit," Gates said, "she should pay me," and left the room without paying.

Carp smiled at Janey, took out one of the bills James Martin, Junior, had just given him, and placed it on the dresser by the door.

He grinned at the whore and said, "I'll be back to work the rest of that off later."

TWENTY-EIGHT

In the morning Clint came down from his hotel room and found McIntyre waiting for him in the lobby.

"Well, what happened to you last night?"

"I got . . . involved with something."

"Something, huh?" McIntyre said. "Is that what you're gonna tell Miranda?"

"What about Miranda?"

"She stayed at the office until late last night, waiting for you to come back."

"I'll apologize to her."

"Sure," McIntyre said, "tell her you got involved with something."

Clint decided to change the subject.

"Are we making that run today?"

"We leave in an hour."

"We have to get two more horses."

"I got them," McIntyre said.

"When?"

"Yesterday."

"How?"

"I used the last of my money to buy them," McIntyre said.

"I was going to buy them," Clint said.

"Makes more sense this way, doesn't it?" McIntyre asked. "My stagecoach, my team, my money."

"What about Miranda?"

"She's got the house and her forty-nine percent, and that's all," McIntyre said. "We get this stage line running, we'll be all right."

Clint didn't want to say what he thought. In a way, the Gold Stage Line was McIntyre's out. Without it, he might go back to drinking heavily. Anyway, protecting the line probably made the old marshal feel even better than owning it.

"We'd better get over to the office and hitch up the team," McIntyre said. "The passengers will start arriving soon."

When they reached the office, Miranda was in the stable, trying to hitch up the team.

"Well," she said as they appeared, "it's about time you two showed up. I thought I was going to have to do this by myself."

"Clint and I will take care of it," McIntyre said. "You'd better go to the office in case some of the passengers show up early."

She wiped her hands on her thighs and nodded.

"All right," she said, walking past them. As she reached Clint she looked at him and said, "I thought you were dead, or something."

"Or something," he said. "I was—"

"Never mind," she said, "you don't owe me any explanations."

She left the stable, and Clint caught McIntyre looking at him disapprovingly.

"What?" he asked.

"You and women," the older man said.

"John—"

"Let's get this thing hitched up," McIntyre said. "I hope I remember how to drive it."

When they had the team hitched, they walked the coach outside and examined it in the daylight.

"Hope the passengers don't mind the patch job," McIntyre said.

"If they do," Clint said, "they can always take the train."

"If they wanted to take the train they would have," McIntyre said. "They'd rather pay our fare than the railroad's, or Wells Fargo's."

Clint examined the two horses McIntyre had purchased the day before. They had hitched them up as the lead two, since they were younger and larger than the other four.

"You approve?" McIntyre asked.

"They're a good-looking pair," Clint admitted, "but they must have cost you a lot, John."

"I had it put away for a rainy day," McIntyre said, "and it was looking pretty damned stormy."

"May get stormier yet," Clint said.

"You think there's gonna be trouble on this run?"

"Don't you?"

"Yep," McIntyre said, "but maybe this will end it. If we're ready for them, maybe it's them who's gonna get a surprise."

"Have we got a shotgun?"

"In the office."

"I'll go and check it out," Clint said.

"I'll get up top and see how it feels," McIntyre said.

"You need a hand?" Clint asked, only half-kidding.

"I can get up onto a coach by myself, thanks," McIntyre said. "Go and take your medicine."

Clint knew what he meant. The shotgun was in the office, but so was Miranda.

TWENTY-NINE

When Clint entered the office, Miranda was sitting behind the desk. She looked up as he closed the door behind him.

"I meant what I said," she told him. "You don't owe me an explanation."

"I know," he said. "John said there was a shotgun in here."

"Oh," she said sheepishly, "yes, it's over here."

She stood up and walked to the wall on his right. The shotgun was mounted there. She removed it, walked to him, and handed it to him.

"It's my father's."

It was an old greener, side-by-side, and a quick, expert examination told Clint that it was in working condition.

"Shell?" he asked.

"In the desk."

She walked around the desk and opened a drawer on the right. There were plenty of shells there, and Clint started removing them and placing them in his pockets.

She expected him to stop after a few, but he continued to remove them, looking for new places to store them on his person.

"How much trouble do you expect?" she asked.

"A lot," he said. "What they did last time didn't work, so they'll try even harder this time."

"But they killed all those people."

"That's right."

"Wait a minute," she said, coming back around the desk. "Do we have the right to expose our passengers to this kind of danger?"

"Probably not," Clint said, "but what would you rather do, fold up your tent? Sell?"

"Selling might not be a bad idea," she said.

"I guess that depends on who you're selling to," Clint said, "but I don't think you'd get my friend outside to believe that, and he's the majority owner. Besides, you don't really want to sell, do you?"

"I don't know what I want to do," she said, resting her firm buttocks against the desk. "Sometimes I think I'd be better off leaving Sacramento altogether."

"Like your father?"

"You know, I held that against my father for a long time, but then I realized that he had earned the right to walk away."

"And you haven't?"

"Not yet, I guess," she said, straightening up. "I'm still here, aren't I?"

He was about to reply when the front door opened and a man walked in.

"Am I interrupting anything?"

Both Clint and Miranda stared at James Martin, Junior, as he stood in the doorway. The silence in the room suddenly became deafening.

"What are you doing here?" Miranda demanded.

"Hello, Miranda," Martin said, smiling.

"I asked what you were doing here," she repeated, harshly.

"I'd like to talk to you, Miranda," Martin said, "alone." He looked pointedly at Clint. "Wait outside, Adams."

Clint looked at Miranda to see what she wanted him to do.

"No," Miranda said, "you stay where you are, Clint." She looked at Martin and said, "Anything you have to say to me you can say in front of Clint."

"Oh," Martin said after a few moments, "it's like that, is it?"

"Just say what you came to say, James, and get out," Miranda said.

"You've changed, Miranda," Martin said. "You've gotten even tougher."

"James," she said, as if very weary, "I heard all you had to say to me a long time ago. Maybe you should just leave right now."

"All right, Miranda," Martin said, "I'll come to the point. I want to buy you out."

"Then Flood was working for you."

"Yes, he was."

"Is the offer still the same?"

"I'll even raise it a little."

"You can raise it all you want, James," she said. "I won't sell to you."

"Miranda—"

"Why do you want this place, Martin?" Clint asked. "Why a run-down line like this?"

"None of your business, Adams."

Clint took a step toward Martin, and the other man took two steps back.

"You will get nowhere brutalizing me," Martin said. "I came alone, and I am not armed."

"Is your father behind this, Martin?" Clint asked. "Or have you suddenly gotten brave and decided to try to make some moves without him?"

Martin looked at Miranda.

"Miranda, this is my last offer."

"Good," she said. "I haven't seen you in years, and if this is your last offer, hopefully I'll never see you again."

"Miranda," Martin said, "this can all be done so easily."

"You heard the lady, Martin," Clint said. "It's time for you to leave."

"All right," Martin said, running his hands over his hair, "I'll leave. You know where to find me, Miranda, when you want me."

"The day I want you," she said, "I'll cut my throat with a dull knife."

Martin flushed, looked at Clint, and then left, slamming the door behind him.

"His last offer," Miranda said.

"He wanted to give you one last chance before we went on this run," Clint explained.

"So what happens now?"

"Now we go on the run, ready for anything."

"What will you do?" she asked. "If you're attacked, I mean."

"Fight them off," he said. "However many they send after us, we'll try to take one of them and find out who they're working for."

"We know who they'll be working for!"

"We need to know for sure, Miranda."

"What if there are too many?"

"Miranda," he said, "if you pay attention to 'what ifs' you'll never get anywhere in this world."

"Clint," she said, grabbing his arm, "let me come with you."

"Why?"

"I want to be there when it ends."

"The real end will come here, Miranda, in Sacramento," Clint said. "What happens out there will just be the beginning of the end."

"Clint—"

"You'll be safer here."

"But . . . what if you don't come back?"

"What did I tell you about 'what ifs,'?" he asked. "Come on, let's go outside and greet the passengers."

THIRTY

As Clint and Miranda stepped outside, they saw three people approaching the office, two men and a woman. One of the men was walking with the woman, who had her arm linked through his, indicating that they were together. They were carrying luggage, which made it obvious that they were passengers.

"You'd better go and greet the passengers, the man and the woman."

"What about the other man?"

"That's not a passenger," Clint said, "that's a policeman."

"A policeman?"

Clint took a moment to dredge the man's name up from his memory.

"Officer Joe Evans."

It was the young officer who had been manning the desk when Clint and Inspector Watson had returned from the site of the coach massacre.

Miranda moved forward to greet the couple, while Clint waited for Joe Evans to reach him.

"Good morning," Evans said.

"Officer Evans, isn't it?"

"That's right," Evans said, "but I'd prefer that you call me Joe."

Joe Evans was dressed in civilian clothes. He was also wearing a holster around his waist. He turned and looked over at the coach, where McIntyre was sitting up top, getting used to the feeling of the reins.

"I see we are about ready to go," Evans said.

" 'We'?" Clint said. "Are you a passenger on this coach?"

"I guess you could say that," Evans said. "The marshal and I had a drink together last night, and I offered him my help."

"What kind of help?"

"I figured that you might need an extra gun on today's run."

"That's right," Clint said, "we could. Can you use that gun?"

"I told you," Evans said. "I used to be a deputy."

"All right, then," Clint said. "Why don't you wait inside until we're ready to leave."

"Right," Evans said. He was wide-eyed with anticipation. "This is the chance of a lifetime, to work with Marshal John McIntyre."

Clint watched the young man spring into the office, wondering just how much experience he really had as a deputy.

"Clint?" Miranda called out.

"Yes?"

"Could we get Mr. and Mrs. Doyle's bags up onto the coach?"

"Sure," Clint said. "I'll take them right now."

He took Doyle's bag, and then reached for Mrs. Doyle's smaller one. Mrs. Doyle, a blonde in her late thirties who was not bad-looking, held on to hers a moment longer than she had to, then caught Clint's eye and smiled.

"Excuse me," he said, and took her bag from her.

"Is he the driver?" Clint heard her ask Miranda as he took the bags to the coach.

"Hey, driver," Clint called, "catch."

McIntyre turned his head just in time to catch one of the bags and stow it up top. That done, he reached down for the other one.

"By the way," Clint said, "your help has arrived."

"What help?" McIntyre asked, frowning.

"You know," Clint said, "that young policeman you had a drink with last night. The one who's very excited about working with the great Marshal McIntyre."

"I still don't know what you're talking about," McIntyre said.

"Joe Evans," Clint said. "Didn't you have a drink with a policeman named Joe Evans last night?"

"Oh, Evans," McIntyre said. "Yeah, we had a drink. In fact, he bought me a drink. That's right," he said, remembering now, "he wanted me to talk about the old days."

"I bet he had to twist your arm."

"Well," McIntyre said, "everyone likes to talk about their better days, Clint—except you fellas who haven't had yours yet."

"Well, he says you asked him to come aboard as an extra gun."

McIntyre frowned again.

"If I did, I don't remember, but it doesn't sound like a bad idea, now that you mention it."

"No, it doesn't," Clint said, "as long as he can handle a gun."

McIntyre was about to reply when he saw something that made him frown even more.

"Now what does he want?"

Clint turned and saw Inspector Watson approaching them.

"Did you see Martin before?" Clint asked McIntyre.

"I wouldn't know a Martin if I tripped over one, but I did see a man go into the office and then come out. I thought he was a passenger."

"That was James Martin, Junior."

"What did he want?"

"I'll tell you that," Clint said as Watson got closer, "after we find out what the inspector wants."

THIRTY-ONE

As Inspector Watson reached the coach, McIntyre stepped down and stood next to Clint.

"I see you gentlemen are getting ready to take a little trip."

"Not a trip," Clint said, "just a run to San Francisco and back. We'll be back tomorrow."

"I should hope so," Watson said. "I wouldn't want to have to come looking for you, Marshal."

"I ain't goin' anywhere, Inspector," Watson said. "I want to clear my name."

"How are you coming on that, Mr. Adams?"

"On what?"

"On clearing the marshal's name," Watson said. "You are investigating Mr. Flood's murder, aren't you?"

"Inspector," Clint said, "we established the first day we met that I wasn't a detective."

"I know that," Watson said, "but the marshal is your good friend. I wouldn't expect you to stand by and do nothing

147

while he is tried for murder."

"I've asked a few questions," Clint admitted. "Why, did someone complain?"

"Not complain, exactly," Watson said, "but I did hear from my superior, who heard from Mr. James Martin that you were bothering—"

"Martin, Senior, or Martin, Junior?" Clint asked, interrupting.

"Well, Senior, of course," Watson said. "Junior is—well, he is not the man his father is."

"Well, my questioning was of Junior."

"Really? Did you find out anything?"

"I'm starting to think that he is not what everyone thinks he is," Clint said. "I'm starting to think that maybe he's starting to acquire a mind of his own."

"Well," Watson said, "I'm sure his father would be glad to hear that. He has always wanted Junior to amount to something."

"But I'm sure he wouldn't consider murder as amounting to something."

Watson smiled at that and said, "You've never met James, Senior."

"No," Clint said, "I haven't, and I don't think I would want to."

"Well," Watson said, "I just wanted to have a little chat with you before you left, just to make sure you didn't have any ideas about not coming back."

"Don't worry about that, Inspector," McIntyre said, "I'll be coming back."

"I hope so, Marshal," Watson said, "I truly hope so. I also hope you'll be very careful out there."

As Watson walked away, McIntyre said, "Now, what do you supposed he meant by that?"

"I think he meant for us to be careful," Clint said. "Here

come some more passengers, driver. You'd better get back
up there."

In all they had four passengers: Mr. and Mrs. Doyle, and
two other men, a whiskey salesman named O'Brien and a
gambler named Mr. Peat. Clint could see that the gambler
was riding a losing streak. His boots were dull, his suit
threadbare, and why else would he be taking a stagecoach
and not the railroad?

When they were ready to leave, Clint went into the office
to get Joe Evans.

"I suggest you don't let the other passengers know that
you're not a regular passenger," Clint said.

"Whatever you say, Mr. Adams."

"And don't do anything until you hear from me, or from
the marshal. All right?"

"I'm here to help, Mr. Adams, and I know how to follow
orders."

"Good," Clint said. "Then let's get under way."

When they were ready to leave, Miranda tried once more
to get Clint to let her come along.

"No, for a new reason," he said.

"What new reason?"

"We have no room."

"Clint—"

"Just sit tight, Miranda, and wait," Clint said. "I have the
feeling it will all be over soon."

At least he hoped so.

When Clint was up top, he stowed his shotgun underneath
the seat, where McIntyre had put a rifle.

"How do you feel?" he asked McIntyre.

"It's been a while," McIntyre said. "The reins feel a little strange in my hands, but all in all I'd rather be here than in jail."

"I think I can understand how you feel," Clint said. "Well, let's head for Rock Springs. If we're going to have trouble, I think it'll come between here and there."

"First time since I can remember," McIntyre said, "that I'm hopin' to run into trouble."

THIRTY-TWO

When James Martin, Junior, left the office of the Gold Stage Line, he went directly to the Lucky Deuce, entering by the back door. In the office he poured himself a brandy and then walked to the door that led from the office to the saloon. He opened the door and waved to Steve Vance, the bartender, who had been watching for him. Vance, in turn, signaled to Carp, who was sitting at a back table.

Carp rose and walked to the office.

"Are you ready?" Martin asked from behind his desk.

"Gates and the others are in position," Carp said. "I just have to ride ahead of the coach and give them the word."

"Well, do it then," Martin said, "and I want the job to be complete."

"You mean . . . you want everyone killed?"

"If you had killed everyone last time, like you were supposed to, this would have been a lot easier."

"Hey," Carp said, "we didn't see Adams."

"Well, see him this time, and kill him."

"Is it really necessary to kill . . . all of them?"

Martin sat forward in his chair.

"You don't understand, Carp," he said. "I'm trying to make a statement, here. Is it a problem?"

"No, not a problem," Carp said, and then added to himself, not for Gates.

Carp remembered the look on Gates's face while he was killing the passengers and the driver. A look of pure enjoyment. Gates didn't look that happy when he was with a woman.

"Then take care of it," Martin said. "Today."

"We'll take care of it, Mr. Martin," Carp said. "I'll get moving right now."

"And do it right, this time," Martin said. "Kill the horses, burn the coach, I don't want anything left. Understand?"

Carp nodded and backed out of the room.

Smiling, James Martin, Junior, poured himself another brandy and wondered what his father would think, or say, if and when he found out that his son was responsible for multiple deaths.

He'd be a proud man, wouldn't he? Even if his son were arrested for murder, a heinous crime to most people, Martin, Senior, would take those murders as a sign of backbone. As for the fact that Martin, Junior, had someone else do the actual killing, Martin, Senior, would see that as a sign of intelligence. As honest as his father was, the younger Martin knew that the man would be proud of him for showing initiative—and in the unlikely event that he was arrested, Martin, Senior, would use his considerable influence to keep his son from standing trial for murder.

This initiative stuff was easy. He should have thought of it a long time ago.

THIRTY-THREE

"How're you doing?" Clint asked.

"It's all comin' back to me," McIntyre called back over the noise of the horses and the coach. " 'Course, this old coach sounds like it's gonna fall apart any minute."

"It'll hold," Clint said. "Remember the beating it took before."

"I remember," McIntyre said, his eyes sweeping the countryside. "You know, if we knew this damned route it'd be easy to guess where they were gonna hit us along the way."

"But we don't know the route," Clint said, "so we'll just have to keep our eyes open."

"You know what I was thinkin'?" McIntyre said.

"What?"

"What if Martin—Junior, or Senior, or whoever's behind this—planted one of them passengers on us?"

"If that's the case," Clint said, "don't forget that we've got a plant inside the coach, too."

"That's right," McIntyre said. "Young Evans."

"Yeah," Clint said, "he is young, isn't he? Yet he says he was a deputy in Wyoming and Arizona."

"Maybe he was."

"Yeah," Clint said, "maybe. He couldn't have that much experience, though."

"As long as he can use his gun."

"He's a big fan of yours, you know."

"So, the boy's got bad taste."

"John—"

"Don't argue with me, Clint."

"Why are you so down on yourself?"

"You remember what I used to think about drunks?"

"Now that you mention it," Clint said, "you hated them."

"Right," McIntyre said. "And what happened? I became one."

"How did it happen?"

"I wore a marshal's star for a long time, Clint. You know that."

"I know."

"And then they took it away from me," McIntyre said. "Said I was too old."

"How old are you?"

McIntyre frowned unhappily and said, "I'm fifty-eight years old. Do you think that's too old?"

Clint formulated his answer very carefully.

"For some things."

"Like what?"

"Well . . . like riding all over the territory on horseback, hunting down outlaws."

McIntyre didn't say anything for a few moments and then said, "So you think I'm too old, too."

"Yeah, John," Clint said, deciding to be honest, "I guess I do."

"Yeah," McIntyre said, "I guess I do, too."

"You do?"

"My head tells me I'm too old for that stuff," McIntyre admitted, "but my heart tells me different."

"I've learned over the years, John," Clint said, "that it's better to listen to your head, not your heart."

"Yeah," McIntyre said, "like if we listened to our heads neither one of us would be here right now, right?"

"You've got that right."

Carp reached Gates and the other men well ahead of the stage. These were the same men he had used the first time, when Adams got away from them.

"This time," Carp said, speaking primarily to Gates, "we don't want him to get away from us."

"Do I get to kill all of them?" Gates asked eagerly.

"All of them."

"Even the old marshal?"

"That's right," Carp said, "even the old marshal."

"What about Adams?" one of the other men asked.

"What about him?"

"He's got a reputation with a gun."

"So?" Carp asked. "There are enough of us to take care of him."

"I don't need any help," Gates said. "I can kill him by myself."

"Maybe you can," Carp said, "but we're gonna be there, so we might as well help."

"Okay," Gates said, "but I want the old marshal." Gates remembered how the marshal had made him back off the other day. "He ain't gonna have no gun under the desk this time."

"He's yours, Gates," Carp promised. He turned to one of the other men and said, "Davis, ride back a ways and watch for the coach. I want plenty of warning when they're coming."

"You'll get it," Hal Davis said.

"The rest of you make sure your guns are loaded and working, and check your horses. I don't want anything going wrong this time. We've got too much money riding on this one."

As the men went to do as they were told, Carp thought, *I've* got too much money riding on this one. He wasn't about to let anyone mess it up for him.

Carp heard someone come up behind him. When he turned, he saw Gates standing there.

"How much money?" Gates asked.

"A lot, Gates," Carp said, "a whole lot."

"A lot for us," Gates asked, "or for them?" He jerked his head in the direction of the other men.

"For us, Gates," Carp said, putting his hand on Gates's shoulder, "for us."

Gates looked at Carp's hand lying on his shoulder and said, "You wouldn't be thinking of cheatin' me the way you're gonna cheat them, would you, Carp?"

"Hey, Gates," Carp said, "we're partners, right?"

"Sure," Gates said, "we're partners. Just as long as *you* remember that, Carp."

THIRTY-FOUR

"Stop!" Clint shouted.

"What?"

"Stop the coach."

McIntyre reined in the team and stared at Clint.

"What's the matter?"

Someone from down below called out, "Why have we stopped?" It sounded like Mr. Doyle.

"Tell him you have to check the horses."

"Just have to check the horses," McIntyre called down. "One of them might have lost a shoe." The older man looked at Clint then and said, "What did you see?"

"I think I saw a rider just atop that rise," Clint said without pointing.

McIntyre looked, but there was no one there now.

"If you did see someone," he said, "he must have been a lookout."

"If that's the case, then they know we're coming," Clint said.

"Well, boy," McIntyre said, "how do you want to play it?"

Clint hesitated and then said, "I've got an idea."

"I kind of thought you would."

Hal Davis rode back to Carp and the others and dismounted.

"They're coming."

"Did you see Adams and the old man?"

"There's an old man driving the stage," Davis said, "and another man sittin' up top next to him."

"That'd be Adams," Carp said. "Let's get into position, boys."

Carp took three men with him, and Gates took the other three. They would attack the coach from both sides, catching it in a crossfire.

Carp was lying on his belly while behind him his men remained mounted. When the coach topped the rise, they would give it time to ride down a ways before they started riding at it from both sides.

As Carp watched, the coach topped the rise and started down the other side. He saw the two men riding up top, McIntyre and Adams.

He got to his feet and ran to his horse.

"This is it," he told his men as he mounted. "Follow me."

Gates recognized McIntyre immediately.

"Here I come, old man," he said. "Get ready to die." He turned in his saddle and said to his men, "Let's go."

As both groups of men started riding down on the coach, McIntyre said to the man next to him, "Here they come. Don't waste a shot."

"I don't intend to," Joe Evans said.

• • •

Riding bareback, Clint hoped that when Martin's men—and he preferred to think of them that way—saw the coach they wouldn't notice that a third-tier horse was missing from the team. Taking the horse was a calculated risk, but Clint couldn't take the chance of being left behind when the action started. Hopefully, Joe Evans would be able to pass as Clint before anyone noticed the difference.

His plan was to trail the coach until the men attacked, and then he would ride up behind them and take as many of them out of the play as he could before they realized he was there. His shots were going to have to be deadly accurate, which under normal circumstances would have been automatic. He had that much confidence in his marksmanship. However, he was not used to riding bareback, and it would take some concentration—and strong legs—to stay astride the animal when it was in full run.

The plan hinged on one crucial point: It would work only if there weren't too many men going against them. With Clint, McIntyre, and Evans shooting, Clint figured they had a better than even chance if the attackers were six or less. Any more than that, and the odds would be long.

As the coach disappeared over the rise, he rode up in its tracks. As he topped the rise, he stopped to watch the action.

Just as he had figured, two groups of men rode down on the coach from both sides, firing their weapons.

As he had feared, there were more than six, but not much more. He counted eight altogether, unless some were being held in reserve.

As McIntyre and Evans started firing back, Clint started down the rise, gun in hand.

THIRTY-FIVE

It wasn't easy for McIntyre to hold the reins with one hand and fire his gun with the other. An experienced driver could have done it with no problem.

Suddenly, McIntyre realized that he wasn't even controlling the team. The horses were running at full speed, and he had nothing to do but hold on to the reins. He decided to tie the reins off, leaving him free to fire more accurately.

Joe Evans was lining up every shot as well as he could. The only rifle they had was with Clint, so McIntyre and Evans had to wait until the men came within range of their handguns. Luckily, the attacking men had chosen to use their handguns as well. As they came into range, Evans sighted down the barrel of his pistol and fired.

Trailing the action, Clint saw one of the attackers thrown from his saddle. He was in the group to the right of the stage, so that meant Joe Evans had shot him. It made Clint feel somewhat better to know that Evans could shoot—as long as it wasn't a lucky shot.

Squeezing his knees tightly to hold on to the horse, he raised his rifle, sighted, and fired at a man from the same group. Without waiting to see what the result of that shot was, he swung his rifle to the group on the other side and fired again.

He swung the rifle the other way and fired again. . . .

Something was wrong.

In a flash Carp knew that something was wrong. The man next to McIntyre didn't look like Clint Adams at all. On top of that, Hal Davis had just been shot out of his saddle, and Carp had been watching McIntyre, and he hadn't fired. The other man was firing on the other side of the coach.

Jesus, Carp thought, and when he turned his head to the right he saw Clint Adams riding a horse behind the coach. He fired again, and suddenly Carp had only one man riding with him. One man . . . and that wasn't nearly enough.

It was time to light out and think of something else.

Right about that time, Gates—who wasn't particularly bright—was getting the same idea. He fired one last shot at the coach and looked around to find that he was alone, and he didn't like it one bit. He was about to wheel his horse around when a shot fired from the coach caught him in the thigh. He held on to his gun but fell from the saddle, landing with a painful thud that knocked the wind from his lungs.

McIntyre saw the last man on his side of the coach turn his horse and run. He grabbed up the reins and tried to stop the runaway team, but they were paying no heed.

"Hang on!" he called to Evans. "They're runnin' away!"

Clint was surprised that their plan had worked so well. He'd managed to kill two men from each attacking group, while McIntyre had killed one and Joe Evans two more. That left one man alive and running, and Clint wanted to catch him and ask him some questions.

The coach team looked as if they were running off, but he decided that McIntyre and Evans would have to deal with that problem. He grabbed a handful of the horse's mane, turned it, and went after the man.

McIntyre kept fighting the team with the reins. Applying the brake at this speed would either do no good, or capsize the coach.

"Have you got them?" Evans shouted, holding on for dear life. From inside the coach a woman was screaming, and men were shouting.

"No, I haven't got them!" McIntyre shouted back, fighting the reins.

"Well, what are you going to do?"

"If you'll stop asking me fool questions," McIntyre said, "I'll get control of them."

"Marshal—"

"Shut up, Evans!" McIntyre shouted back. "Just shut up!"

Jesus, McIntyre thought, you're tryin' to save somebody's life—and your own—and they're yappin' at you.

He wished the people inside the coach would shut up, too.

Clint never would have caught the man if his horse hadn't stumbled and fallen, throwing the man to the ground. Clint's coach-weary mount never would have caught up to him. Now, as he reached the man, whose horse had run off, he slid to the ground as the man was picking himself up.

Clint stepped in and kicked the man in the chest hard enough to knock him back down but not hard enough to hurt him.

"Hey . . ." the man said, weakly.

"I'm going to ask you some questions," Clint said to the man, "and I'm only going to ask each question once."

"Whataya doin'—" the man started, getting up again. Clint kicked him again in the chest, harder this time, knocking him down again.

"Stay there," Clint said.

They both seemed to realize at the same time that the man still had his gun in his holster. Clint could see in the man's eyes that he wanted to go for it, and if he did, Clint was going to kill him.

"Go ahead," Clint said, "do it."

The man thought about it a moment and then relaxed, resting on his elbows.

"What's your name?"

"Carp."

"Carp," Clint said, "here come the questions, and remember, I'm only going to ask you once. . . ."

By the time Clint walked the man back to the coach, McIntyre had regained control of the team, and the coach was standing still. The passengers had stepped outside and were milling about.

"Who do we have here?" McIntyre asked.

"This is Carp," Clint said. "Have you ever seen him before?"

"Yep," McIntyre said, squinting to get a better look, "I sure have. He was in my office with Flood and the other man, Gates."

"Yeah," Clint said, "he told me he worked for Flood and that he now works for Mr. Martin."

"Junior or Senior?" McIntyre asked.

"That's the funny part," Clint said. "He's taking money from both of them."

McIntyre started to laugh. Clint turned to say something to Carp, and while his back was turned Gates limped out from behind the coach, blood soaking his entire left leg from the thigh wound. He had raised his gun and was prepared to fire when Joe Evans saw him.

"Marshal!" Evans shouted.

McIntyre turned, drawing his gun. As Clint turned away from Carp, he saw McIntyre fire. The bullet struck Gates in the chest and dropped him to the ground.

McIntyre holstered his gun and turned to look at Clint. "Too old, huh?"

Clint shrugged and said, "Did I say that?"

THIRTY-SIX

When Clint walked into James Martin, Junior's, office the next day, Brenda Loring looked up from her desk at him and smiled.

"Well," she said, "where have you been? It's been a whole day."

"I've been busy," he said. "Is Junior in?"

"Yes, but he's in with his father."

"Is that the door to to Daddy's office?" Clint asked, pointing.

"Yes, but—"

Clint walked to the door and opened it. Martin Senior, was seated behind his desk, and Martin, Junior, was standing in front of it.

"Who are you?" Senior asked.

"Pa," Junior said, "this is Clint Adams."

"Ah," Senior said, sitting back in his chair, "Mr. Adams. What can I do for you, Mr. Adams?"

"Nothing, sir," Clint said, "I'm here to talk to your son."

"About what?"

"Business."

Martin, Senior, looked surprised.

"You doing business with my son?"

"I guess you could say that."

"We're not doing any business together," Junior said.

"Yes, we are," Clint said, "sort of."

"I don't understand," Senior said.

"Maybe if you let us talk, and just listened, you would understand."

"Very well," James, Senior, said, "talk."

"I have nothing—" Martin, Junior, began, but Clint cut him off.

"The men you sent after John McIntyre and myself yesterday are dead, Mr. Martin," Clint said. "All but one. Carp is alive, and in the hands of the police."

"Carp?" Martin, Senior, said.

"Yes," Clint said, "the man who was working for both you and your son."

Both Martin, Senior, and Clint fell silent, awaiting a reply from James, Junior.

James, Junior, did not know quite what to say.

"Come on, man," Senior said, "what's your reply?"

Junior looked at his father and then at Clint.

"What would you like me to say?"

"I don't know," Clint said. "Carp has told the police it was you who hired him to attack the Gold Stage Line and kill all of the people."

"What?" Martin, Senior, said.

"The first time," Clint said, "and then again yesterday. Unfortunately for them, yesterday we were ready for them."

Again they seemed to be waiting for James, Junior, to reply.

"James," his father said, "is this true?"

Junior looked at his father and said, "Yes."

"But . . . why, man?"

"Why, to make you proud, of course, Father."

"To make me proud," Senior asked, "you caused the death of . . . how many people?"

Junior looked at Clint and asked, "How many?"

"Six people from the first coach, including a child, plus the driver," Clint said, "and seven of the men you hired—"

"I wasn't counting them," Junior said, looking pleased. "That's fourteen, isn't it?"

"Fifteen."

"Hmm?" Junior said.

"Let's not forget Flood."

"Ah yes," Martin, Junior, said, "Flood." He looked at his father and said, "And I did that one myself. I was walking past his window and there he was."

"Why did you kill him?" Clint asked.

"He was becoming difficult," Martin, Junior, said. "He wanted more money, or he was going to tell my father what we were doing."

"And what were you doing?" Clint asked. "You certainly didn't become partners just to try to buy the Gold Stage Line."

"No, we were buying a lot of business," Martin, Junior, said, "even if they didn't want to sell."

"You were strong-arming people into selling you their businesses cheap."

"That's what Flood was for," the younger Martin said. "He was good at that."

"And you were after the Gold Stage Line for what reason?"

"I wasn't after the line," he said, "I was after Miranda."

"You figured if she didn't have the line she'd come to you?"

"Of course."

"Then you don't know her very well, James," Clint said. "Come on, let's go."

"Where?"

"To the police."

"You think I'm going to the police with you?"

"You are," Clint said. "Carp has already confessed that you paid him to commit murder."

"My word against his."

"You are also going to clear John McIntyre of Flood's murder."

"Let him hang."

"You're coming with me," Clint said, "one way or another."

James Martin, Junior gave Clint a pitying smile.

"If I know my father, he's already taken steps to take care of you, Adams."

Clint looked at James Martin, Senior.

"Have you done that, sir?" Clint asked. "Have you taken steps to have me taken care of?"

"I have," Senior said. "There's a hired gun waiting outside. On my signal from this window, he will kill you."

"And will you give him that signal?"

Martin, Senior, looked at his son, who was wearing a smug look, and said, "I don't think so."

"What?" Junior said, momentarily shocked. Then he looked at Clint and said, "Then I'll go with you, because he'll use his money to get me off."

"Buy you off a murder charge?" Clint asked. "I don't think even your father would be foolish enough to try that . . . would you, sir."

"Quite the contrary, Mr. Adams," Senior said. "I could certainly do that. . . ."

"See?" Junior said.

" . . . if I wanted to," Senior finished.

"But?" Clint asked.

Senior looked at Junior and said, "I'll use my money to get you a good lawyer, James, but I won't buy your freedom. I can't."

"What?" Junior said. "Pa, you can't be serious about this."

"But I am," Senior said.

"Jesus, I'm only doing what you would have done," Junior said. "I was doing business exactly the way you do it."

"I don't kill people, James."

"No," Junior said, "you hire it done."

"Is that what you think of me?" Senior said. "I'm sorry, James."

"What are you doing to me?"

"What I should have done a long time ago," Senior said. "I'm making a man out of you."

James, Senior, looked at Clint and said, "Take him to the police, Mr. Adams. Clear your friend. I'll be along with his lawyer."

"Come along, James," Clint said.

"Pa," Junior said, giving his father a pleading look, "you can't mean this."

But he did, and once more, justice was served.

Watch for

FIVE AGAINST DEATH

123rd novel in the exciting GUNSMITH series
from Jove

Coming in March!

NELSON NYE

The Baron of Blood & Thunder

Two-time winner of the Western Writers of America's Golden Spur Award, and winner of the Levi Strauss Golden Saddleman Award . . . with over 50,000,000 copies of his books in print.

NELSON NYE

Author of RIDER ON THE ROAN, TROUBLE AT QUINN'S CROSSING, THE SEVEN SIX-GUNNERS, THE PARSON OF GUNBARREL BASIN, LONG RUN, GRINGO, THE LOST PADRE, TREASURE TRAIL FROM TUCSON, and dozens of others, is back with his most exciting Western adventure yet. . . .

THE LAST CHANCE KID

Born to English nobility, Alfred Addlington wants nothing more than to become an American cowboy. With his family's reluctant permission, Alfred becomes just that . . . and gets much more than he bargained for when he gets mixed up with horse thieves, crooked ranchers, and a band of prairie rats who implicate him in one crime after another!

Turn the page
for an exciting preview of
THE LAST CHANCE KID
by Nelson Nye!

On sale now,
wherever Jove Books are sold!

My name is Alfred Addlington. Some may find it hard to believe I was born in New York City. I never knew my mother. Father is a lord; I suppose you would call him a belted earl. The family never cared for Mother. Marrying a commoner if you are of the nobility is far worse, it was felt, than murdering someone.

I was, of course, educated in England. As a child I'd been an avid reader, and always at the back of my mind was this horrible obsession to one day become a Wild West cowboy. I'd no need to run away—transportation was happily furnished. While I was in my seventeenth year my youthful peccadillos were such that I was put on a boat bound for America, made an allowance and told never to come back.

They've been hammering outside. I have been in this place now more than four months and would never have believed it could happen to me, but the bars on my window are truly there, and beyond the window they are building a gallows. So I'd better make haste if I'm to get this all down.

I do not lay my being here to a "broken home" or evil companions. I like to feel in some part it is only a matter of justice miscarried, though I suppose most any rogue faced with the rope is bound to consider himself badly used. But you shall judge for yourself.

Seventeen I was when put aboard that boat, and I had a wealth of experience before, at nineteen, this bad thing caught up with me.

So here I was again in America. In a number of ways it was a peculiar homecoming. First thing I did after clearing customs was get aboard a train that would take me into those great open spaces I'd so long been entranced with. It brought me to New Mexico and a town called Albuquerque, really an overgrown village from which I could see the Watermellon Mountains.

I found the land and the sky and the brilliant sunshine remarkably stimulating. Unlike in the British Midlands the air was clean and crisply invigorating. But no one would have me. At the third ranch I tried they said, "Too young. We got no time to break in a raw kid with roundup scarce two weeks away."

At that time I'd no idea of the many intricacies or the harsh realities of the cow business. You might say I had on a pair of rose-colored glasses. I gathered there might be quite a ruckus building up in Lincoln County, a sort of large-scale feud from all I could learn, so I bought myself a horse, a pistol and a J. B. Stetson hat and headed for the action.

In the interests of saving time and space I'll only touch on the highlights of these preliminaries, recording full details where events became of impelling importance.

Passing through Seven Oaks, I met Billy, a chap whose

name was on everyone's tongue, though I could not think him worth half the talk. To me he seemed hard, mean spirited and stupid besides. He made fun of my horse, calling it a crowbait, declared no real gent would be found dead even near it. Turned out he knew of a first class mount he'd be glad to secure for me if I'd put one hundred dollars into his grubby hand. He was a swaggering sort I was glad to be rid of. Feeling that when in Rome one did as the Romans, I gave him the hundred dollars, not expecting ever to see him again, but hoping in these strange surroundings I would not be taken for a gullible "greenhorn."

A few days later another chap, who said his name was Jesse Evans, advised me to steer clear of Billy. "A bad lot," he told me. "A conniving double-crosser." When I mentioned giving Billy the hundred dollars on the understanding he would provide a top horse, he said with a snort and kind of pitying look, "You better bid that money good-bye right now."

But three days later, true to his word, Billy rode up to the place I was lodging with a fine horse in tow. During my schooling back in England I had learned quite a bit about horses, mostly hunters and hacks and jumpers and a few that ran in "flat" races for purses, and this mount Billy fetched looked as good as the best. "Here, get on him," Billy urged. "See what you think, and if he won't do I'll find you another."

"He'll do just fine," I said, taking the lead shank, "and here's ten dollars for your kindness."

With that lopsided grin he took the ten and rode off.

I rode the new horse over to the livery and dressed him in my saddle and bridle while the proprietor eyed me with open mouth. "Don't tell me that's yours," he finally managed, still looking as if he couldn't believe what he saw.

"He surely is. Yes, indeed. Gave a hundred dollars for him."

Just as I was about to mount up, a mustached man came bustling into the place. "Stop right there!" this one said across the glint of a pistol. "I want to know what you're doing with the Major's horse. Speak up or it'll be the worse for you."

"What Major?"

"Major Murphy. A big man around here."

"Never heard of him. I bought this horse for one hundred dollars."

"Bought it, eh? Got a bill of sale?"

"Well, no," I said. "Didn't think to ask for one."

I'd discovered by this time the man with the gun had a star on his vest. His expression was on the skeptical side. He wheeled on the liveryman. "You sell him that horse?"

"Not me! Came walkin' in here with it not ten minutes ago."

"I'm goin' to have to hold you, young feller," the man with the star said, pistol still aimed at my belt buckle. "A horse thief's the lowest scoundrel I know of."

A shadow darkened the doorway just then and Jesse Evans stepped in. "Hang on a bit, Marshal. I'll vouch for this button. If he told you he paid for this horse it's the truth. Paid it to Billy—I'll take my oath on it."

A rather curious change reshaped the marshal's features. "You sure of that, Evans?"

"Wouldn't say so if I wasn't."

The marshal looked considerably put out. "All right," he said to me, "looks like you're cleared. But I'm confiscatin' this here horse; I'll see it gits back to the rightful owner. You're free to go, but don't let me find you round here come sundown." And he went off with the horse.

"Never mind," Evans said. "Just charge it up to exper- ience. But was I you I'd take the marshal's advice and hunt me another habitation." And he grinned at me sadly. "I mean pronto—right now."

Still rummaging my face, he said, scrubbing a fist across his own, "Tell you what I'll do," and led me away out of the livery-keeper's hearing. "I've got a reasonably good horse I'll let you have for fifty bucks. Even throw in a saddle— not so handsome as the one you had but durable and sturdy. You interested?"

Once stung, twice shy. "Let's see him," I said, and followed him out to a corral at the far edge of town. I looked the horse over for hidden defects but could find nothing wrong with it; certainly the animal should be worth fifty dollars. Firmly I said, "I'll be wanting a bill of sale."

"Of course," he chuckled. "Naturally." Fetching a little blue notebook out of a pocket, he asked politely, "What name do you go by?"

"My own," I said. "Alfred Addlington."

He wrote it down with a flourish. "All right, Alfie." He tore the page from his book and I put it in my wallet while Jesse saddled and bridled my new possession. I handed him the money, accepted the reins and stepped into the saddle.

He said, "I'll give you a piece of advice you can take or cock a snook at. Notice you're packin' a pistol. Never put a hand anyplace near it without you're aimin' to use it. Better still," he said, looking me over more sharply, "get yourself a shotgun, one with two barrels. Nobody'll laugh at that kind of authority."

"Well, thanks. Where do I purchase one?"

"Be a-plenty at Lincoln if that's where you're headed. Any gun shop'll have 'em."

I thanked him again and, having gotten precise directions, struck out for the county seat feeling I'd been lucky to run

across such a good Samaritan. I was a pretty fair shot with
handgun or rifle but had discovered after much practice I
could be killed and buried before getting my pistol into
speaking position. So Evans's advice about acquiring a
shotgun seemed additional evidence of the good will be
bore me.

It was shortly after noon the next day when I came up
the dirt road into Lincoln. For all practical purposes it
was a one-street town, perhaps half a mile long, flanked
by business establishments, chief amongst them being the
two-storey Murphy-Dolan store building. I recall wondering
if this was the Major whose stolen horse Billy'd sold me,
later discovering it was indeed. Leaving my horse at a hitch
rack I went inside to make inquiries about finding a job.

The gentleman I talked with had an Irish face underneath
a gray derby. After listening politely he informed me he was
Jimmie Dolan—the Dolan of the establishment and could
offer me work as a sort of handyman if such wasn't beneath
my dignity. If I showed aptitude, he said, there'd be a better
job later and he would start me off at fifty cents a day.

I told him I'd take it.

"If you've a horse there's a carriage shed back of the
store where you can leave him and we'll sell you oats at
a discount," he added.

"I'd been hoping to get on with some ranch," I said.

"A fool's job," said Dolan with a grimace. "Long hours,
hard work, poor pay and no future," he assured me. "You
string your bets with us and you'll get to be somebody while
them yahoos on ranches are still punchin' cows."

I went out to feed, water and put up my new horse. There
was a man outside giving it some pretty hard looks. "This
your nag?" he asked as I came up.

"It most certainly is."

"Where'd you get it?"

"Bought it in Seven Oaks a couple of days ago. Why?"

He eyed me some more. "Let's see your bill of sale, bub," and brushed back his coat to display a sheriff's badge pinned to his shirt.

I dug out the paper I had got from Evans. The sheriff studied it and then, much more searching, studied me. "Expect you must be new around here if you'd take Evans's word for anything. I'm taking it for granted you bought the horse in good faith, but I'm going to have to relieve you of it. This animal's the property of a man named Tunstall, stolen from him along with several others about a week ago."

I was pretty riled up. "This," I said angrily, "is the second stolen mount I've been relieved of in the past ten days. Don't you have any honest men in your bailiwick?"

"A few, son. Not many I'll grant you. You're talkin' to one now as it happens."

"Then where can I come by a horse that's not stolen?"

That blue stare rummaged my face again. "You a limey?"

"If you mean do I hail from England, yes. I came here hoping to get to be a cowboy but nobody'll have me."

He nodded. "It's a hard life, son, an' considerably underpaid. Takes time to learn, but you seem young enough to have plenty of that. How much did you give for the two stolen horses?"

"One hundred and fifty dollars."

He considered me again. "You're pretty green, I guess. Most horses in these parts sell for forty dollars."

"A regular Johnny Raw," I said bitterly.

"Well . . . a mite gullible," the sheriff admitted. "Reckon time will cure that if you live long enough. Being caught with a stolen horse hereabouts is a hangin' offense. Come along," he said. "I'll get you a horse there's no question about, along with a bona fide set of papers to prove it. Do you have forty dollars?"

I told him I had and, counting out the required sum, handed it to him. He picked up the reins of Tunstall's horse, and we walked down the road to a public livery and feed corral. The sheriff told the man there what we wanted and the fellow fetched out a good-looking sorrel mare.

"This here's a mite better'n average, Sheriff—oughta fetch eighty. Trouble is these fool cowhands won't ride anythin' but geldin's. I guarantee this mare's a real goer. Try her out, boy. If you ain't satisfied, she's yours fer forty bucks."

The sheriff, meanwhile, had got my gear off Tunstall's horse. "Get me a lead shank," he said to the stableman. Transferring my saddle and bridle to the mare I swung onto her, did a few figure eights, put her into a lope, walked her around and proclaimed myself satisfied. The animal's name it seemed was Singlefoot. "She'll go all day at that rockin' chair gate," the man said. "Comfortable as two six-shooters in the same belt."

Thanking them both, I rode her over to the nearest café, tied her securely to the hitch pole in front of it and went in to put some food under my belt, pleased to see she looked very well alongside the tail-switchers already tied there.